Pacific Gold

By

Al Holzman

Copyright 2010   Allen B. Holzman

Cover photos by Leslie Chandler Holzman

All rights reserved. No part of this book may be reproduced stored or transmitted by any means without written permission of the author, except ion the case of brief excerpts used in critical articles and reviews.

Printed in the United States of America
First published 2010

This is a work of fiction.

The author may be reached at:
www.straitaero.com

Pacific Gold

To: Shipmates Leslie & Thelonius

With thanks to Dennis K. Biby, author of
<u>Moloka'i Reef</u>

Al Holzman

Pacific Gold

CHAPTER 1: Cliff House

* *0830 3 October   Pos: approx. 1 mile offshore Crs: South   Spd: 4 knts   Dpth: 30 fathoms Wx: drizzly rain, big seas   Helmsman: Beth Comments: Broad reaching under main, mizzen & jib.*

"Cliff House is gone," Beth said in a flat voice as she tucked a stray wisp of brownish-blonde hair under her seaweed green Sou'wester. The tone of her voice matched the sullen, dull, ache in my gut.

A cross–swell from starboard slapped the hull amidships, "Whump." The wind was down, the rain slacking off, the leftover seas were big and sloppy.

I stared shoreward at the sea cliff. Through the misty rain it looked the same as always, except of course, for the new scar where the slide had been--and the house was indeed gone. Gone, as though it had never existed. If I was seeing this piece of the Oregon coast for the first time, I wouldn't know the difference today from yesterday. The house hadn't been a stalwart, landmark mansion built on the brink to defy the elements. No, it was a modest (small), shake sided, weathered gray-brown, two-story house of the style erected a hundred years ago by people without bank accounts.

"Whump!" Another swell collided with the hull amidships. I ducked back under the hatch as the sea sloshed over the rail into the cockpit rewetting Beth's yellow rain pants.

"So," she said, gazing at the spot that was empty of the house we used to live in. "A good day for beachcombers."

My stare dropped to the base of the cliff where the surf crashed onto the new mound of dirt and rock rubble. No sign of the house though. I searched the high tide line in either direction. "Yeah, it must be--although I don't see anything that looks like house debris."

"Whump!" Another wave splashed into the cockpit. The drains gurgled as the sea ran back out. "So, Captain Jack, do you think maybe we could change course a little so more of these swells stay in the ocean instead of jumping into my lap?"

I wanted to say, "Do what you want." But I didn't. Instead I said, "Yeah, good idea. Let's get into deeper water. It should be smoother out there. No point in staying near this coast. The harbors are closed anyway."

The Coast Guard station had displayed two red pendants, signifying gale warnings when we sailed by at oh-dark-thirty. They might have stopped us, but it was raining hard (and I had neglected to turn on the running lights.) So we slipped through a crack in the Coasties vigilant effort to protect us from ourselves. Beth commented as we bashed through the first set of breakers over the bar, "Slipping is a lot better than falling through a

Pacific Gold

crack." I guess the Coasties didn't think anybody would leave a nice, secure harbor on such a nasty morning.

It *had* been breaking over the bar, but only because the tide was at full ebb. I explained that to Beth and she said she didn't see where that, "made a foaming farthing's difference."

Her comment had broken the tension that had been building for hours(days? years?) Or perhaps it was the rush from breaking out to freedom. I laughed--we both laughed as we crashed through the second set of breakers into the big ocean outside.

"You've got to cut back on those romance novels." [Beth reads buccaneer novels with lurid pictures on the covers of half naked men (handsome) defending sexy, pale, (voluptuous) ladies wearing torn dresses aboard burning pirate ships. (I have never read one--maybe out of fear that I'd get hooked on them too.)]

"Oh yeah? What would I read? Bowditch? I might lose your place and you'd have to start over."

I had been reading, "The American Practical Navigator" by Nathaniel Bowditch, for about a year and was nearing the middle of volume one. "No, no, we wouldn't want that. If I lost my place we'd have to go back to the harbor and start over."

"I hope you've read enough to get us back *into* a harbor."

Our mood had sobered again as we looked at the place where the house had been.

Now, Beth moved the tiller to port, bringing the boat onto a west-south-west heading which brought the wind abeam and the swells onto the starboard bow. The rolling abated to a rhythmic pitching with seas occasionally slopping onto the fore deck. It also brought the ex-house site around to the stern port quarter directly into my line of vision but behind Beth.

Something symbolic there I suppose. And rightfully so. The house only entered her life five years ago when we moved to Oregon. It had been my heritage forever--maybe longer... eighty years before I was born Frank and Olga Astor (no known relation to the famous Astoria Astor) built what came to be known as, "the Old Astor Place".

Originally Frank built his house at least a quarter mile from the sea. It was your usual, single family, two story, four bedroom (three up, master down), no bath, dwelling in the forest. (If Laura Ingalls Wilder had written about it, the book would have been titled, "Little House in the Cold Rain Forest" or possibly, "Little House in the Big Briar Patch".)

Frank wasn't a Timber Baron, or a Mining Magnate, or a Sea Captain. No, but he was the first of a line of Oregon Stump Farmers named Astor. (A stump farmer is a man who gets a plot of timber land and slowly logs it off; selling the trees and farming between the stumps that are left behind. He gets a cow or two, some chickens, and takes on incidental jobs, construction, logging, mill work, fishing, etc... to support the *farm*.)

Anyway, Frank (fortunately) built his house on the east side of his property and logged west to the sea. Over the next hundred years the sea gradually ate away Franks farm until all that was left of the Old Astor Place was the Old Astor House. And then, last night, it took that too. (Of course Frank is long dead. The sea had gotten to him earlier--he had been buried in the back forty west of the house.)

"The Sea giveth and the Sea taketh

Pacific Gold

away," my Uncle Milford, the lay preacher, is fond of saying. I never could see what the sea gave, except maybe a view. The Astor family remained "stump farmers" even after the sea took the *farm*. (Except me. Except me? I got away--I think.) Maybe though, in the guise of taking, the sea did give us something. First it gave us freedom from the farm, and then, finally, last night it freed me from the house and all remained of the Astor Place.

Beth pulled in the main and mizzen sheets a bit, trimming the sails for our new heading. "Would you like me to take up the jib sheet a little?" I asked. (The main and mizzen sheets are easily adjusted from the helm, the jib sheet is more difficult.)

Beth squinted at the foresail and replied, "Yeah, if you don't mind."

"I'll be right out." I grabbed my rain jacket from the hanging locker beside the companionway and shrugged it on--glad to have some activity--some diversion from my gloomy introspection. Climbing out into the cold damp breeze and fitting the winch handle into the port sheet winch, I made the most of the simple task. After uncleating the sheet I slowly cranked the winch with my right hand while keeping tension on the tail of the line with my left. Beth watched the sail, and finally gave her nod of approval.

"OK...No, ease it off a bit."

I let the sheet slide slowly over the barrel of the winch.

"There. That looks good."

I cleated the sheet off. Looking aloft I checked over the sails. No holes, no loose track slides, tight luffs, trimmed a little too close for my taste--but that's the way Beth likes them. My hand itched to pop the main sheet out of its jam cleat and slack it just a bit. But no, she would resent it.(I guess I would too if I had the helm.) It doesn't do to criticize the set of someone else's sails. Besides, we're not out for an afternoon's race. What does a fraction of a knot or a half degree of heel matter when you're looking at months, maybe years, of sailing? Not nearly as much as your partner's good will. Not a "Foaming Farthing's etc..." I chuckled to myself as I settled back against the cabin bulkhead.

"What's funny?" Beth asked with a touch of defensiveness in her tone.

"Ah," I stalled, with an appreciative sigh. "It just feels good to be gone. And I suppose," I added truthfully a moment later. "Good to know that the house is gone too."

"Mmmm yes," She nodded her agreement. "It was an interesting place to live. Fun really. Except when it shook from the surf beating on the cliff at night." She paused a comfortable pause. We were speaking slowly, as people do when they have all the time they need to say exactly what they mean. "You're right, it does feel good to be gone. To be free of the entanglements, all the webs and roots, all that interpersonal history crap. There was just too much history in that place. Too many ghosts. Not that any of it meant anything. Not that any of it was worth..." her voice trailed off.

"A foaming farthing!" I volunteered with a laugh.

She laughed too, "Yes dammit! A Friggin' Foaming Farthing! Now that you mention it, I do feel really free." She smiled her mischievous smile (the one I had fallen in love with.) "Free enough to pee over the side. Take the tiller!"

"Aye, aye." I scrambled aft while checking the sails and wind again. "Maybe the winds

steady enough to let the wind–vane take over."
"Whatever. Just don't touch those sheets." (She knew--of course.)

Standing on the cockpit bench she unfastened the shoulder straps of her rain pants and shucked them off to the rhythm of the pitching boat. Then she scurried forward along the high side of the deck in her pink long underwear. I watched, wondering if a wave would give her a bath before she got around the front of the cabin and into the relative safety on its lee side. It didn't and she did. Looking aft she commanded, "Avert your eyes."

I turned to engage the wind–vane.

Chapter 2: At Sea

- *0600 7 October   Crs: South   Spd: 5 knts
Dpth: O.S. (off soundings)   Wnd: NW 10–15
Wx: Dark w/ stars   Helmsman: R.L.S.
Comments: Broad reaching under full sail –– Beth sleeping*

    R.L.S.? Robert Louis Stevenson. Was he any good on the helm? Did he ever steer his own boat? He must have––at least a little––though he didn't have to––yachting was a lot different then. For one thing, you had to be rich. Rich enough to hire a crew anyway; no homeless waifs of the waves.
    Morning thoughts. Predawn thoughts. Soon the sun will melt away the darkness and the real world will solidify again. But for the moment we are sloshing along in a small dark world. Some have likened it to a womb, but at this latitude it's a cold mother.
    Why RLS? Why not RLS? Maybe his spirit is up there riding on the spreaders. His health went down the toilet; my home fell into the ocean; we both headed for the South Seas.

Pacific Gold

"So RLS," (I picture him up on the spreaders wearing his three piece Scottish sailing suit.) "Tell me Sir, are we on course for Vailima? That is, heh, heh, Vailima via Treasure Island?"

In the darkest of predawn darkness I am wide awake, cold, standing on the bridge deck, leaning back against the mizzenmast staring up at the mainmast's spreaders that I can almost see. I (almost) see RLS up there with one hand on the port shroud and one on mast, dancing a little Scottish jig and saying, "Aye Matey! Treasure Island first! Heh, heh! Then Vailima. Then maybe Vailima. Aye, Aye, Matey! But beware of the Black Spot! Steady as She Goes!"

Treasure Island? Yes, Treasure Island! That's where this little ship of dreams is bound. Treasure Island. Our, *almost*, secret destination.

Our discovery of Treasure Island was accidental. Beth and I had moved into the Old Astor Place on the cliff when my sister's husband, Walter, refused to live there anymore. He claimed he couldn't sleep because the house shook too much when the surf was up and crashing into the cliff below. Said he was afraid of waking up in the surf. He couldn't swim.

"I can swim," I said to tweak him a little. So, after finding a job within driving distance, we moved in. (Beth has often said that if we'd been living anywhere but North Dakota, she would have checked it out first. But she didn't and we did––move in.)

Anyway, it was a dry summer when we moved in. The roof didn't leak until the fall rains began. We were sleeping in one of the upstairs rooms that first night of the rains. I woke up to dripping sounds and a wet bed. Next morning, after a big breakfast (bacon, eggs, hash–browns, toast with homemade marion berry jelly, and freshly ground coffee,) we ventured up into the attic.

The dim light that came through the louvers on either end revealed a rough plank floor covered with approximately a hundred years worth of dirt, bird, bat, and/or mouse shit, and enough pots, pans, coffee cans, and buckets to outfit a couple of kitchens. Each was strategically located under a leak in the old shake roof. The only real problem with the system was that some were rusted through and self emptying. Apparently Brother-in-Law Walt, and probably my father before him, hadn't thought that a new roof was a good investment for an old house destined to fall into the ocean.

"Well," I said to Beth, "It looks as if our relatives let the roof go back a bit."

"A bit, perhaps," she agreed. "Or maybe they had other plans for the attic? If we pull off a few more shingles we could have a large communal shower room featuring organically pure rainwater."

"That's an idea, and in the summer it could be a solarium."

"Sure. And at night it could be a lunarium. We'd be overrun with Yuppies."

"We could open a Bed and Bath and Breakfast! A B&B&B! It would be a sure fire draw. But the rainy season is not a good time to be opening new businesses on the Oregon Coast--or changing roof styles."

"True. A person wouldn't want to slip and fall off the wrong side of this roof. Not without a really good life-preserver anyway."

"Perhaps, we should just dump some of these leak control devices." I made my way over to the nearest louver, thumbed back the rusty, bent nails that were holding it in, and removed it.

Pacific Gold 15

"I suppose the trick is to remember where they are so we can get them back in the right places."

Beth picked up two overflowing coffee cans, (Folger's and MJB,) "No trick there, they've made their marks." Each can had left a nice rust ring on the floor.

We slogged back and forth leaving barefoot prints in the mud and bird-bat/rat shit on the plank floor. We noted that aluminum sauce pans worked better than coffee cans, but cut-off plastic bleach bottles were the best--especially if they were cut off leaving the handles.

Removing the louver had the added benefit of letting in more light which made it easier to maneuver through the cans and pans on the floor. It also revealed a pile of stuff that had been pushed under one of the eves. The pile was haphazardly covered with old plastic dry-cleaner bags.

"What's all this?" Beth asked, prodding the pile with her toe.

I shrugged my shoulders and continued hauling, emptying, and contemplating roof solutions. (The dry-cleaner bags initiated a train of thought concerning the use of plastic, a sort of under-the-rafters plastic tent, which when implemented, worked fairly well for the last few, precarious, years of the house's life.) Beth cautiously delved into the stack and wrenched out an old suitcase. The handle came half off in her hand as she did. It was your common '50's suitcase; imitation alligator hide cardboard, with rusted hinges and locks, a couple of decals, a large water stain, and a mouse hole in one end. When the clasps wouldn't unclasp, Beth pried them off with a broken pot handle. "Hmmph, looks like a bunch of old letters," was her disappointed comment. "I thought it might be full of money or at least neat old dresses."

She picked up a ribbon bound packet of slightly mouse chewed envelopes and squinted at the faded return address in the dim light. "These are from Randolph Astor. Who is he?"

"He was one of my Uncles who died in World War Two; in Europe I think. Is there a date on the postmark?"

She thumbed towards the middle of the packet to a less faded envelope. "Yeah, this one's October, 1943." Going back to the suitcase she picked up another bundle. "How about William?"

"Another Uncle. Died in North Africa. Grandma was a three time "Gold Star Mother". The third one was Carlyle––he died in the South Pacific."

She picked up the remaining bundle. "Yes. Here he is." She studied the last bundle. "Good Grief, did she lose all her boys in that war?"

"No, Dad and Uncle Milford came back, but the Astors did their bit for our freedom."

Later, (after all the drips were being caught and containered again,) downstairs by the wood stove, we pieced together and read the highly censored war letters from my dead Uncles.

We had finished Randolph's and William's bundles. A lot of Uncle Randolph's were missing due to the mouse, but William's were fairly complete. Both bundles had ended with a letter from the War Department which began, "We regret to inform you..."

Beth refolded William's "We regret..." letter and put it on his stack. "Pretty sad stuff," she commented and sighed. "I think I've had enough for now."

Pacific Gold

"These should be different," I said, breaking the rotted ribbon that held the third bundle together. "Carlyle wasn't a combat soldier. He was a SeaBee. And, from what everyone said, he was a little *different*. I think that he was more of an adventurer type."

She was gazing out the window at the gray rainy day fading to evening. "Oh well, I suppose that we might as well finish." Moving towards the kitchen she asked, "Do you want anything?"

"Yeah, how about another beer?" I put down the letters, stretched, and put some more wood on the fire.

When she returned with cheese, crackers, beer, and etc... we resettled and began on Carlyle's correspondence. His letters were different. Grandma must have been relieved to get them. Where William and Randolph had written of dreary mud and sand, miserable heat and/or cold; Carlyle wrote of pretty beaches, tropical flowers, warm moonlit nights, and impossible dreams and schemes. His letters weren't as badly mutilated by the censor's scissors, (although time and weather had done a pretty good job on some of them.) The war didn't seem to be more than a small cloud on Uncle Carlyle's horizon and wasn't prominent in his letters.

Actually it was Beth who discovered Treasure Island. We were deep into Carlyle's bundle, my eyes were about shot from deciphering his faded writing. I was in the kitchen getting another beer, (a Stout this time.)

"Hey! Listen to this!" Beth called from the living room.

I pried the top off the bottle and stood in the kitchen doorway. She carefully smoothed the letter on the worn linoleum floor. "Ah, let's see...here it is...listen to this, Carlyle writes,'...great news! After this war is over my fortune is made. I made a discovery today that will take care of me for a long time. I can't say more, but believe me it's good!' That's all he says. I wonder what he found?"

I came and looked over her shoulder, reread what she had read. "I don't know. No one ever mentioned Carlyle's fortune to me. Probably just another whacky idea."

We didn't really expected to find any answers, but he had piqued our interest and we quickly deciphered the rest of the stack. About three letters before the final one, the one from the war department, we got our answer.

He was in the Western Pacific by that time and things weren't fun. He wrote that he was in a field hospital, *"down with a bit of a fever." Of course he expected to be up and around shortly--but, just in case he wasn't, he wanted Grandma to know about a dream he'd had. He wrote, "...I dreamed that we were working on an island in the Dangerous Archipelago. The little island was a part of the Sea Gull Group. We were building an airstrip. There was just enough room on the motu for the runway. I was down in a big hole. I think we had dug it for a foundation or something under the southeast corner of the runway--right under where the airplanes would touchdown. I was finishing up, cleaning the last of the sand off the coral bedrock when I saw what looked like two golden potatoes. They were stamped with some kind of a crest and Spanish words. The Sergeant called and I had to climb out quick as they were wanting to start dumping truck loads of coral rock into the hole. The noise of falling rocks woke me up, but of course it was not rocks--just the sound of artillery going off..."* He wrote a couple more pages and then added, *"P.S. That dream I had reminded me of a letter I wrote to you about 18 months ago."*

There were a couple more letters but no further mention of fortunes or dreams. Then the final War Department's, "We regret..." letter. But Carlyle's was different than the others. They regretted that Carlyle was *missing in action*; rather than *killed in action* as William and Randolph had been.

Beth and I labeled the motu "Treasure Island."

Thinking about it now, it's hard to believe that rainy day was five years ago.

So that is where we are headed, Treasure Island!

Chapter 3: Perils of the Sea

- *0700 8 October Crs: South Spd: 4 knts
Dpth: O.S. Wnd: 10 knts NW
Wx: Clear & Sunny! w/ fog-bank to west.
Helmsman:Wind Vane
Comments: Sunshine is much, much better than fog.*

- Sunrise. The warm golden rays gently eased the damp chill that had settled in my bones. Soon the cockpit was littered with cast-off rain gear, damp socks, damp sweat shirt, damp mitts, damp etc., etc... The cool air made the sun's warmth precious; like the heat in a cool sip of *Chevas* on the rocks. The first Sun of the voyage! A fog bank loomed threateningly to the West, but we were bathed in Sunshine. Glorious Golden Sunshine!

    "Bang!" The companionway door slammed open to reveal Beth squinting out into the brightness. "Hey! What's going on out here? Ow, what's with this brightness?" Her hair was all over the place, a pillow mark indented the

Pacific Gold

side of her face, but her expression was bright. She climbed out into the cockpit and stretched.

"Good morning. Sleep well?"

"Oooo god. Like a dead person." She gazed out over the gently rolling, sparkling blue-green sea. Inhaling a deep breath of sea air, she tilted her face back towards the sun and arched her back. "EEEEyeaaaah."

Leaning back on the cabin, "How was your watch?"

"The best. Beautiful sunrise; then the warmth arrived."

"It must have been pretty devastating. This cockpit looks like a garage sale," she commented sniffing disdainfully at the scattered clothing. "Well, gotta go pee." She jumped up, turned to go forward, and stopped.

"Whoa, would you look at that." She was staring at the menacing fog bank to the west. "Is it moving in or moving out?"

"Neither. It just seems to be sort of waiting there."

"Well, don't do anything to make it curious," she said and stared forward again.

"Right. Pee off the sunny side." I went below to build a pot of coffee.

The stove was going and the water heating when Beth joined me in the galley.

"Mmmmm, that smells good." She sniffed the aroma of the coffee grounds in the filter. "Pancakes or Oatmeal?"

"Cooks choice. Both sound great. Nothing like fresh air and a lack of food to build up the old appetite."

She rummaged around in the pot and pan cupboard and came out with the frying pan. "Pancakes."

Then in a more sober tone she commented, "At least no one is following us."

"No? Why do you say that?"

"Well, I didn't see anyone, did you?" She bent down, lit the second burner, turned it up, and covered it with the pan. "It's so bright and all, I should think we'd see if anyone were following us."

"That's true, I guess the storm may have worked in our favor." I didn't think she had taken me seriously (or for that matter the whole Treasure Island idea) when I had insisted on leaving quietly.

Early on she had told our secret. We (I) had bought the boat, Hispaniola, about a year after finding the letter. Beth was unenthused and unimpressed when I said that we needed a good sea boat if we were going to go after the treasure. (She thought we should just fly down.) Actually Hispaniola wasn't very impressive and needed a lot more than TLC, but the price was right and I thought I could fix her up. (It took two plus years, but I did fix her up--mostly.)

Anyway, Beth was unhappy about it and told a couple of girl friends at work about the boat and sailing to Treasure Island. She didn't say where it was or anything, just that I had bought an old wreck of a boat and thought that I was going to sail there and get rich. A couple days later Bully Hansen ambled out of a bar and confronted me about it. I was pretty unhappy about that and let Beth know. Treasure Island had been a touchy subject ever since. Actually, it wasn't a subject at all; it wasn't mentioned again. But, when the time finally came, we both knew why I didn't want a *Bon Voyage* party.

"Well, maybe everyone's forgotten about Treasure Island by now--if anyone really took it seriously to start with," I tried to normalize the whole subject. After all, if we were really going to find the damned island we'd probably

Pacific Gold

have to talk about it.

She gave me a questioning look.

"I'm sorry I made such a big thing about it back then. But still, when you're going treasure hunting it's probably not a good thing to advertise it, unless you want company."

"You've had experience?"

"I read the books," I said with a grin.

"Hah! I've read more books about buried treasure than you'd believe," she paused significantly, slopped some olive oil onto the frying pan, winked, and continued. "And you're right. I know that I should have said it a long time ago, I'm sorry I blabbed. Especially now, since we're really on our way." She spooned some batter into the middle of the puddle of smoking oil. "We *are* headed for the Dangerous Archipelago, aren't we?"

"Aye Matey! Steady as she goes--down the coast, then we'll hang a right and sail across the big ocean to the Sea Gull Islands in the Dangerous Archipelago."

"Whew, I wish I'd of kept my big mouth shut. I never thought we'd really go. It's creepy to think that someone might be watching us."

"Yeah, well, we'll have to be careful and remember to glance over our shoulder from time to time. It's a big ocean. After we pick up our visas in San Francisco, it should be easy to disappear over the horizon."

Beth moved a stack of pancakes onto a plate and handed it to me. She re-oiled and rebattered the pan as I buttered and syruped my breakfast. "More coffee?"

I nodded with a full mouth.

She refilled my mug. "So, where to after San Fran?"

I swallowed pancakes and sipped coffee. "Mmmm, good breakfast. After Frisco our options are wide open. We can continue on south to San Diego, or Mexico; further if we feel like it. Or, we can head southwest from there and leave this continent behind. The only rub comes if someone were to guess that T. I. is in French Polynesia. There are a limited number of Ports of Entry and it wouldn't be hard to find out if we're there."

Beth flipped her cakes. "Well, I didn't say which ocean it's in. At least I wasn't that stupid."

"That's good. I guess we'll know if and when the time comes to worry." All the same I had an over-powering urge to be outside and have a look around the horizon. "I think I'll finish my breakfast out in the sunshine."

Beth loaded another stack of pancakes on my plate as I squeezed past her back side. "Good idea, I'll join you in minute."

A quick glance around confirmed that we were still alone, the sun still shining, and the fog-bank still looming off to the west. I didn't really think anyone had the least interest in what we were doing, but...

After breakfast we washed the dishes in the cockpit, and then ourselves.

"God, it's nice to be clean and warm and dry, again." With the towels flapping from the rigging we lounged in the shelter of the cabin with the sun warm on our pale skins. Beth pulled a handful of her honey blonde hair over her face and smelled it. "Especially clean hair. I always feel better after I wash my hair."

The wind picked up as I took the noon sight. Beth put a reef in the main while I worked out our position.

Before dark I tied in the second reef. The fog rolled over us like a wet carpet. We seemed to be rocketing through the night even though the knot meter showed we had slowed to five

Pacific Gold

knots. I kept watch until ten, then Beth took over.

"Whew, dark out here."

"Yeah, about as dark as it gets, but I can still tell if my eyes are open or shut."

"Course still South?" She checked the compass. "Anything to run into up ahead?"

"Not that I know of. I haven't seen any lights from any ships."

"Good. It is kind of nice to see them. Then at least I know where they are, and it gives me something to look at besides the compass."

"I guess I'll sleep some, let me know if the wind picks up, or whatever."

"Oh don't worry about that," she said with a smile in her voice. Then more seriously, "Captain Jack? Do you really think we'll find the treasure?"

I shrugged my shoulders in the dark. "Maybe, maybe not--but it seems like a worthy venture. If nothing else it's a good excuse for a nice boat ride."

"That's what I think. We might as well give it our best shot."

"Sure. Either way it'll be more fun that way. We'll have to keep our heads about it though and not go crazy."

"Yeah, especially if we find it."

I lay awake listening to the occasional wave slosh on deck and the surging rush of the water on the other side of the inch and half mahogany hull planking. Not for the first time, I allowed myself to think about finding the treasure and what it might mean to our lives. What would it be like to be rich? How rich? Then my mind shifted to dangers and difficulties--bad guys and pirates.

I must have rocked off to sleep because the next thing I heard was Beth's voice. "Oh God!

Al Holzman

Jack! Jack!!!!"

I bounded out of the bunk and up the companionway steps. Beth was pointing forward, her mouth and eyes wide with terror. I turned to see a red light to starboard, a green light to port, and a large black space between them dead ahead. The lights were well above the bow so they had to be close and mounted on something big!

I dove into the cockpit and pushed the tiller hard over to port. Hispaniola slewed around to starboard. "Sheet in!" I yelled as the cross-swell slapped over the bow and plastered us with spray.

Beth leapt into action hauling on the jib sheet as I hauled in the main. Hispaniola heeled sharply and accelerated--almost as though she knew the danger that she was in.

Steering with one hand, I hauled in the mizzen with the other. By then we were surfing on the freighter's bow wave away from a black wall of cold steel.

The ship rumbled on by and disappeared into the foggy mist. I started breathing again and slowly turned Hispaniola back onto a broad reach. Beth eased the sheets. "Good," I responded each time a sail was where I wanted it. Beth cleated them off. Slowly my death grip relaxed on the tiller and the wind vane took over again.

"Wow..." My legs and hands were shaking, and my teeth wanted to chatter.

"Jeez Jack, I'm sorry."

"It wasn't your fault. Those guys were going really fast. You can't see through fog. They should have seen us on their radar. Damn! They never knew we were there."

"I was just shining the flashlight on the jib. I thought that it was flopping. Then I saw the green light come out of the fog. I looked to go left, but when I looked around the sail--there was the red light. That's when I freaked. God!" She stopped and shuddered. "Look at me, I'm still shaking."

"Hah! Look at me, I'm naked!"

Chapter 4: San Francisco

- *0600 13 October Crs: ESE Spd: 4 Knts   Dpth: O.S.
WX: Dark, patchy fogs Wnd: NW light
Helmsman: W.V.
Comments: Big city, small world*

"Light Ho," Beth said softly from her perch in the companionway. The wind-vane was steering as we rocked gently through the night.

I was just beneath the thin edge of sleep. Without opening my eyes I asked, "What kind of light?"

"White flashing land light."

Opening my eyes I consulted the telltale compass mounted over the bunk. One hundred degrees, just right. Reluctantly I crawled out of the warm bunk and pulled on jeans, sweat shirt, rain jacket, and watch cap. I picked the wristwatch off its hook in the galley, before climbing the companionway steps to squeeze up

Pacific Gold

beside Beth.

"Right about there." Beth pointed off the port bow. I saw a dim white flash. "There it is."

I nodded yes, zeroed the stop watch, and timed the interval between flashes. "Five seconds. Point Reyes Light. Right where it's supposed to be. And if it is," I turned to starboard and crouched low to see under the genoa sail. "The Farallons Light should be over here." After a bit I saw a weaker flash. "Ah, right on. There it is." I timed the new light. "Fifteen seconds--I'll check the chart just to be sure I'm right."

I slid down into the cabin to confirm the lights. It was true; we were right where I thought/hoped we would be. A little thrill went through me--it's nice to be right when you're not sure that you know what you're doing.

After building a pot of coffee, I rejoined Beth in the companionway hatch. We snuggled close, sipping the strong French roast, as the sky slowly pinked up separating it from the darkness of the land. "Land Ho."

"Land Ho, and we've left the fog behind."

"Yes, that's the best news of all." Looking aft I saw the long, low, fog-bank off to the west looking like another continent. "Thank You."

"Who are you thanking? The fog-bank for letting us go?"

"Perhaps, but not really. I suppose that I was really thanking the *God of the Wind and Sky and Sea and Everything Else.*"

"I see. And does this God have a name?"

"No. But maybe yes. I suppose It could have lot's of names. Different names in different places."

"Hmmm, like YAHWEH?"

"Perhaps, but certainly not Jehovah. Jehovah is too young. Maybe just GWaSaSaEE?"

"Gwa-sa-saee...hmmm...nice ring to it. Gwasasaee, sounds Aztec or something. Ten years of marriage and you've never mentioned this personal deity before."

"We've never really been at sea before."

She cocked her head to one side. "Ah,....A Sailor God."

We lapsed into silence as the sun sent its first precious rays through the cool dawn to touch our faces.

It was afternoon when we rode the flood tide under the Golden Gate Bridge. The space between the pilings seemed narrow after two weeks at sea, especially with an outbound tug boat plowing through at the same time.

Then we were looking at the impossibly narrow opening in the breakwater that is supposed to be the entrance to the San Francisco Yacht basin. Land was closing in fast.

Beth took over the helm. I cranked the diesel, then went forward to drop the sails, tie on the fenders and push them over the rail. We were approaching the opening at, what seemed to me, breakneck speed. I stifled the urge to yell back to Beth, "Slow Down!" I knew that wouldn't be cool (Captains aren't supposed to yell at their Crew, especially if they're married to the Crew.) Beth easily guided Hispaniola though the entrance, down the jetty and into the slip area.

"Now what?" she called, slipping the transmission into neutral.

I studied the lay out in front of us and walked back to the cockpit so that we could confer without the dreaded yelling. "How about if we just end–tie on that finger?" I suggested, pointing to a pier end. "Then we can go see the Harbor Master and he can assign us a slip."

"Sounds good to me," she responded. "Port or starboard?"

I shrugged, "Ladies choice?"

She studied the empty space at the end of the dock. "Well, into the wind would be best...so, starboard it is."

"Aye, aye. Steady as she goes."

"Do you want to take her in?" Beth asked suddenly, eyes wide.

"No, I'll tend to the dock lines. Take it slow and we'll be fine."

Looking back at our proposed parking slot she said, "OK." And reached down decisively with her left hand to slip the transmission from neutral to forward leaving throttle at idle.

As the boat chugged forward Beth pulled the tiller over initiating a sharp starboard turn in preparation for a big sweeping turn to port which put us gently alongside the dock.

I tossed the bow line to a sailor on the dock. He said his name was Gybe, and invited us aboard his boat Ferrity for a beer after settling with the harbor.

Beth shut down the diesel and we ambled up the dock with our sea-legs rolling under us. The Harbor *Mistress* said we would be just fine where we were for a few days, gave us shower keys in exchange for a twenty dollar deposit, and we were back outside in the gentle San Francisco sunshine. The grass was green. The air smelled like springtime. Life was good.

We went back down the dock to have that beer and chat with Gybe.

The next few days were filled with shopping for boat things; spare blocks, stove parts, shackles, etc... And stocking our larder with a six month supply of essentials and as many perishables as we could eat before they went bad. We also made a couple of trips over the hill to the French consulate to secure visa's for French Polynesia.

Al Holzman

Finally, I couldn't leave San Francisco without a trip to Golden Gate Park to see the Rodin sculptures and Beth had to pay her respects at the Zoo. We had overcome our big city paranoia enough to enjoy the long bus ride out for a whole day of leisure and recreation.

It was dusk when I stepped off the bus back at the Yacht Basin. I turned to give Beth a hand as she stepped down when I heard, "Wall lookee thar. If it ain't me ol' bud, Jacky Asss–tor." I went cold. Beth took my hand and stepped out. "An' the lovely Missus Asss-tor ta boot."

Beth stopped. The bus doors hissed shut behind her. In the silence and exhaust fumes the bus left behind, Beth said, "Hello Bully. What are you doing here?"

Bully was leaning his two-hundred-and-fifty–plus pounds of muscle, fat, and bull-shit against a convenient light pole. His dirty "Cat" ball cap was pushed back on his head, he shifted the match stick in his mouth from port to starboard. "Wall, isn't that some way to greet an ol' frien' who's come all the way down hair to the big city jist to he'p out."

(I'd known Bully since first grade. His real name was William Hansen. His name had changed from Billy to Bully early on, probably in that same first grade, and it was appropriate. Bully never helped anybody without helping himself.)

We stood frozen in the awkward silence, Bully, leaning against the light pole, Beth, tiredly clutching her string bag full of odds and ends from the day of fun, me, completing an unequilateral triangle--kind of stuck in between them. It felt like some mythological formation of stones, frozen in time at a dusky moment of eternal awkwardness--three rocks in

Pacific Gold

a river.

The street light flickered on. "I have to take this stuff to the boat," Beth stated, turned and walked off stage left, towards the pier. The lime-stone shattered.

Bully watched her stride off. "What'd you ever hook up with that stuck up Bitch for anyway?" He turned toward me. "Guess she must be a good piece, huh?"

"So, just how were you planning to help out?"

"Ho!" he snorted. "Ain' you the one. No messin' aroun'. No, 'How ya doin' Ol' Buddy? Good ta see ya.' I come all the way down here jus' to hep ya out, as a favor ya ain' even asted for, an you treats me like this. You mus' get it from that Bitch wife. All ya wants ta know is what Ahm gonna do for You. Ah got a good min' ta jus' leave, an' let ya fin' thins out for yur sef."

Bully talked real slow in a low gruff voice using a dialect all his own. He varied the dialect to suit his obscure purposes.

I wanted to tell him, "Buzz off." And go on down to the boat, locking the dock gate behind me as I went. But he wouldn't go away. He would just be more obnoxious. Bully has a great capacity for obnoxiousness. I wasn't afraid of him, but he *was* intimidating (he wasn't called Bully for no reason). I just didn't have the energy to deal with him.

The gate to the dock banged shut. Beth walked over to the restrooms. I waited.

Bully scratched the stubble on his chin with his thick thumb-nail. "The Missus checkin' up on ya, huh?" He favored me with a leer and an oversized wink. "Hey, why don't you show me your boat?" He suddenly changed his tack, dropping his dialect in a burst of enthusiasm.

"You saw it back home. It hasn't changed."

"I never seen inside. What's a real sailboat like inside anyway? It must be pretty nice if you can live in it for weeks at a time. How many people can sleep in that thing anyway?"

Beth came out of the restroom and walked over. "So what's going on?" she asked.

"Nothing much," I replied. "I was just thinking of going down the street for a beer, want to come along?"

She shrugged her shoulders. "Sure."

"Ah could use some liquid refreshment mesef." Bully drawled. "Lead the way an I'll buy the firs' roun'."

Bully bought the first round, of course, forcing me to buy another––but that was OK. I had regained my balance with Beth sitting close beside me at the rickety little table, and I was curious about what Bully had alluded to. I decided to wait and see where he was going with this. I could wait.

It didn't take long. Bully was about half-way through his second beer when he said, "You guys sure left a mess behind when you split like that." He took another swig. "Not that I blame ya none. I'da prolly done the same mesef."

"What are you talking about?" Beth asked.

He squinted at her like he wanted to spit on the floor. Finally he said, "Why that house of yourn an all. When it fell off'n thet cliff it just splattered all over. Hell of'a mess. Chamber of Commerce boyos all upset...whooee!...and them Eee Pee Aye pogies. Whooee! Theys a-fit ta be tied. Yessiree Bung-ho-Babee! They be a-lookin' for you-uns right this here momento." Smacking his lips he shook his head. "Whooee." He killed his second beer in a mighty gulp, followed by a belch to match.

"Now wait a minute," Beth said. "We didn't push that old house off the cliff. The cliff fell out from under it. We didn't do anything wrong. And what the hell is an ee pee aye?"

"Wall, that's the way I'd see it, if'n it were me. But it ain't me. It's them guv'ment queers. Them en-viron-men-tal dip-wads. An' they sees it differnt." He sat up and looked around the bar room as though they might be right there.

I signaled the waitress for another round while glancing around to see if anyone was taking exception to Bully's loud use of the word *queers*. "No, it ain' me," he continued conspiratorially. "It's them. An they're a sayin' you–uns shoulda hauled it away afore the cliff gave out. Yessiree, thets a what theys a sayin'." He dropped his big head down woefully with his long, stringy brown hair swaying back and forth as he shook it.

"Well, that's just plain silly," Beth asserted indignantly.

The waitress arrived. Bully grabbed a beer off her tray and had it half drunk before I got the tab paid. I was beginning to see a plan. I paid her double and asked for another round right away.

"Yessiree. The word is there's a ree-ward out for you two."

Beth stared at him. "Really? How much?"

"Reeeally." Bully smirked and took another drink. The waitress brought the next round. Bully had his eyes on her cleavage as she placed the bottles in the middle of the table. He slammed his nearly empty bottle down with a great belch and grabbed another.

"How much?" Beth persisted.

He took a slow, almost meditative drink, and then said, "Oh, couple a thou each, I spose....I didn't actually see it fer mesef. I jus hightailed it down here ta warn ya."

Beth took a petite sip from her glass, and

asked brightly, "So what's your grand plan?"

Bully smiled voraciously. "Wall naow Little Britches, I was justa comin' ta thet." He paused significantly. I took the occasion to have a big, obvious, drink. He couldn't resist, not that he wanted to, having a bigger one. In fact he killed another bottle. After ritually belching, wiping his stubbly chin with the back of his hand, and taking possession of a new bottle, he continued, "Yessiree Booby, as soon as I heeard about the ree-ward I figgered you uns was fixin' ta get into trouble. I jus' had ta hightail it down here ta warn ya."

He fondled his next bottle of beer. The table was getting so full of bottles that it was hard to tell the full ones from the empties. So, just for effect, I traded my empty for another empty carefully wrapping my hand around it above the label so he couldn't tell. (My deviousness was probably wasted, but my alcohol level had reached that point of extreme mental clarity.) I glanced at Beth--*she* had noticed. I hoped it tipped her off to my strategy.

"Well, thank you. It was very considerate of you come down and warn your old school chum. So that's your plan?" Beth pressed on.

I winced at the thought of being Bully's chum.

Bully grinned wolfishly at the praise. "Oh, anybody woulda done thaat--thet thought of it, that is. Thas the trouble you see--mos people doan' think." He tapped his head significantly. "But there's more. Yessirree Baby! There's more." He took another drink and winked in my direction. "Yessirree Booby!" (I sensed Beth cringing.) "I dint come har to jus put the scare into ya. I come ta hep ya. I'm gonna go with ya!" He announced with a wave of his hand that knocked a couple of empties off the table.

I had been afraid that would be his big plan.

It wasn't hard to get the waitress' attention, she was picking up the empties off the floor. I signaled for another six beers. She was reluctant. I begged with my eyes. She shrugged one shoulder and headed for the bar.

I turned back to the table as Beth asked incredulously, "Go with us? Where?"

Bully gave out a whoop, and shouted, "Why, to get the treasure, Lil' Darlin'!" He clamped his big hand over his big mouth and glanced around the room like he'd accidentally let the cat out of the bag. He dropped the hand and guffawed into her perplexed face. "Haw! Haw! Haw!"

The waitress brought the six new beers. Not wanting her to take away the empties, I pushed some of them aside to clear a space where Bully would have clear access. She set down the full bottles and cleared the empties anyway.

Beth mumbled something about the "little girl's room", and left the table. A little unsteadily, I wondered if she was going to throw-up.

"Nice ass," Bully commented as he watched her walk away. "Hope ya doan' mind me complimentin' yer ol' lady but she do have a good lookin' ass--pretty fair tits too. Course they could be padded some, ya never know."

"Hmmm yeah," I commented noncommittally. "I'd say the bar maid's are sure enough the real thing though."

Bully swiveled around to where the barmaid was clearing another table--there weren't many people left in the pub. "Yeah, now thas the truth. Ain't hidin' nuthin' in that outfit. Ah like the way she smiles." He guffawed a couple of times and slapped my shoulder. "Remember that ol' joke? Ah think Ah'll jist ask her where she's sleepin' tonight."

"Hah! You better have a couple more beers and forget it. She's probably got a big boy friend just waiting to kick your butt."

Bully looked away from the barmaid's backside and narrowed his eyes at me. "Ain't none of these here city slickers gonna kick ol' Bull's ass. An I'll sniff out that little piece if'n I've a mind to."

"Hey, go for it."

"Right." He chugged another beer. "Right after I have a piss." He struggled to get out of his chair and wandered off in the general direction of the men's room. He passed Beth on his way and clumsily tried to pat or pinch her bottom as they passed. She let out a little yelp and jumped away.

She came over to the table, "Did you see that?" I nodded sympathetically. "Well that's it. I'm out of here. And that ass–hole is not getting on our boat either."

"Hey, I'm with you. Go back to the boat. Get everything ready to go. I'll be along as soon I can ditch him."

"Are you kidding? Sail tonight?"

"Why not? We don't have any reason to stay, do we?"

"Well no, it just seems kind of sudden is all." She glanced around and saw Bully coming back. "OK, just don't be too long––and don't you dare bring him!" She whispered hoarsely.

"You can count on that. Now give him a dirty look and get going." I nearly patted her bottom, but thought better of it.

She did as I asked but the look was wasted as Bully was veering off in the barmaids direction. He didn't make contact though. She had stopped at a table with customers. Bully kept going and wound up back at our table. He slopped into his chair and grabbed a fresh bottle of beer.

"Goddamn, missed her. Hey, what's happened ta yer ol' lady? She take off er sumptin'?"

"Yeah, I guess she didn't care much for your attention to her backside."

"Hah, a little pinch? Jus bein' friendly like. They all like it. 'Specially them that the act like they doan! Trust Ol' Bull on that'n. Like this Bitch, she's just achin' fer some special 'tention like Ah'm fixin' ta give her." He chugged down his beer. "Hey, drink up and let's get another roun'. I'll buy this'un." He slewed around in his chair. "Hey, Beer-maid! A couple a bars for me an my ol' bud here!" He turned back to me and said confidentially, "Jus you watch ol' Bull work here."

"Right," I said, getting up and slapping his shoulder. "You get to work, but I just gotta have a pee."

I met the waitress as she came around the end of the bar with the fresh beers. "Say," I stopped her. "Could you do something for me?"

"Depends," she said, raising her eyebrows.

"Could you keep him occupied for about fifteen minutes?"

"It'll cost you."

"How much?"

"Dollar a minute."

"It's a deal." I pulled out my last twenty. "How about a half-hour?"

She took the money.

I headed for the restroom--and kept on going straight out the backdoor. I tripped over a bum on the back step, he yelled something, but I

was on my way.
    As I jogged the beer sloshed in my belly and the lyrics of an old song bounced around my brain, "...and run for the harbor, that's the life of a Sailorman."

Pacific Gold

Chapter Five: On The Run

- *0000,19 October Crs: Various   Spd: Unknown
Dpth: 10 feet to 20 fathoms Wx: Dark w/ beer fog
Helmsman:B & J
Comments: Running with a belly full of beer is never easy.*

"All set?" I puffed out as I plodded to a halt on the dock by the boat.

"Aye, aye, Captain, cast off at will."

"Right-o Matey. At Will, not at Charlie--or Bully." I muttered as I uncleated the mooring lines. Suddenly I realized that I *really* had to PEE. I threw the lines on board, gave the boat a mighty shove, and hopped on deck. We were away, sliding quietly through the water towards the harbor's entrance--while I peed off the bow sprit. (How do *you* spell relief?)

With considerable satisfaction I tucked in and headed back towards the cockpit. "Perhaps you should crank up the diesel?" Beth tactfully suggested as she guided Hispaniola in the general direction of the exit hole in the breakwater. "Or raise a sail? Or something? That was a good push, but I don't think that it is going to get us clear of the breakwater."

"Oh yeah. Right," I said, sniffed around for wind in the darkness. "It was a good push though. Not Homeric, but jolly good." I detected a slight land breeze. "We've got a bit of a breeze, how about if we save fuel and sail?"

"Whatever, just do it soon. We're running out of steerage and the rocks are getting closer. I imagine Bully is too."

"Right," I dashed to the bow, barked a shin on the Sampson post, unbagged the genny, freed the halyard, and hoisted the sail. Unfortunately the sheet was still jumble on the fore deck. Fortunately the breeze was just a breeze. The sail flapped gently to windward over the starboard rail. I stomped on the bitter end of the sheet before it slipped over the rail, jerked the sail in, and cleated off.

I felt like throwing up as I collapsed against the cabin bulkhead. "Oooh," I groaned and rubbed my shin. "I'll never let Bully buy me another beer."

"I hope that he doesn't have the opportunity, but I think you were doing most of the buying."

Just then a coon-dog's wail came from the direction of the marina. Then, "Jaaack Asssturrrd, youuu sorrry son--of--aa--biiitch!! Aah'lll git youuu forrr thisss!" This was followed by the sound of a trash can getting the shit kicked out of it and the barking of a real dog.

"Nice guy," Beth commented as we slid quietly into San Francisco Bay.

"Right. Not exactly my idea of a good shipmate."

Beth shivered. "That's when I get off."

I drug myself to my feet as the boat rocked in the bay swell. "Guess I might as well raise the main and mizzen."

"How should I steer?"

"Straight on. That flashing light is Alcatraz. Maintain whatever compass heading *straight on* is. The current will push us to the west. If Bully is watching, he'll think we're heading out to sea. When we get beyond Alcatraz we'll turn." I was busy taking sail ties off the main as I plotted our escape strategy.

"OK--but, isn't that what we are doing? Heading out to sea?"

I found the halyard and shackled it to the head of the mainsail. "I'd rather not. Unless you feel strongly about it, I'd like to get some sleep before heading offshore." I finished tightening the shackle. "Slack the mainsheet a bit, please."

"Sleep sounds good to me," Beth replied and yawned as she popped the mainsheet out of its jam cleat. "How do you propose to do that?"

I hauled the big sail up the mast with the halyard and returned to the cockpit. "Well, we could nip into Sausalito, which is just inside the Golden Gate Bridge (on the north side). I wouldn't want to do that in the dark though. And if there's any place Bully might look for us, I suspect that would be it. Angel Island is a state park with mooring balls. It's off to the northeast aways. It would be good, but if the government really is looking for us it probably wouldn't be smart to register at a state park. The third choice, and the one I'm favoring, Treasure Island."

"Not *thee* Treasure Island?"

"Unfortunately, no. This little island is

under the Bay Bridge. There's some kind of military facility on it, but there's also a cozy little bay where we should be able to get a good, undisturbed, days sleep."

"That sounds good. Bully would never think of looking for us at a military installation. Besides, I like the name... You're sure that its OK to anchor there?"

"Yes, but if it isn't, I think the worst that would happen is they would ask us to leave. We may be wanted for littering, but I doubt that we'd be suspected of spying."

"Hmmm, speaking of littering. Do you think it's true?"

"Good question. It sounds hokey, but I'm not so sure Bully'd be capable of making it up. It sounds like something that came out of the Bay Front Bar. But on the other hand--it does sound a bit like the E.P.A."

"I think that if there is a reward out on us, Bully would have turned us in. He didn't seem too sure on that part."

The breeze had picked up and we were sailing along at a nice five knots or so. The current pushed us, as predicted, west towards Alcatraz. I reached down into the cabin and flipped on the navigation lights. (No sense in stirring up the Coast Guard.) The fresh air and activity had cleared my brain to where I didn't feel drunk anymore, just very tired.

"Well either way, it seems like a good time to leave the country for awhile."

"Ditto for sure."

We found Treasure Island. Darkness wasn't a problem because dawn was well broken. It was a simple matter to sail in and drop the anchor in twenty feet of water. We were the only boat in the the little cove but, more interested in privacy than amenities, we

Pacific Gold

anchored well away from the little crescent of sand.

I tidied up the topsides while Beth fried up some bacon and scrambled eggs with cheese--we skipped the coffee.

I awoke listening to the traffic on the Bay Bridge. I don't think the distant sounds of tires, horns, and motors woke me--it was just there when I returned to consciousness.

Cars, trucks, and busses, rushing back and forth like ants on a log. Been there, done that--wore out the tee-shirt. I'd rushed back and forth across this very bridge, hardly noticing this little island. It's hard to believe that it was in this same lifetime. It wasn't really. I had a different wife, a different mind--a *job*. Had there been someone anchored down here then? Probably. Some one lying in bed, naked, with his woman, semi-awake in the middle of the afternoon, listening to the ambitious ants hurrying to oblivion.

Yeah. Been there. Neared the brink of oblivion and turned left--took an off ramp in the middle of life's freeway.

Bull-shit. I'm still headed towards oblivion--everyone is. Yeah, but I'm not longer hurrying.

Hmmmm, maybe we should be. We might be fugitives--on the lam from a giant littering charge--a price on our heads. What's the fine for massive littering? Ten thousand? Twenty? What does it matter if I don't have it. Take my house?!!

I chuckled out loud. Beth stirred in her sleep, burrowing a little deeper under the covers.

Yes, take my house--but not my boat. Sobering thought. No boat--no *Treasure Island*.

Maybe we ought to be getting out of here. Off into the sunset--over the horizon--under the rainbow. Don't forget to snag the pot of gold on our way by. Yes!

It's always raining under a rainbow. (Who cares? I've got a raincoat.) (Yay, though I sail through the valley of the rainbow, I will fear no wet--for I've got a raincoat!)

Whoa. Time to get moving. No time to be sacrilegious. Time for a change of mind. Time to get Sailing!

I carefully eased out of bed, used the head, pulled on a pair of sweats, and went on deck.

The sun was in the west--three o'clock, maybe. It looked to be about half-tide and rising. This would be a good time for sailing. But no, I'd rather go in the morning with the whole day ahead of us. Besides there was the little matter of the the shower keys and moorage.

By my reckoning we owed the harbor master, over at the yacht basin, thirty-three dollars. I don't believe in running out on moorage fees. I just might need to come back some day and besides, it just wouldn't be right. (Code of the West? Perhaps.)

So, the key deposit was twenty, the keys and a check for thirteen dollars would square us.

I eased down into the cabin, found my checkbook (still had a few dollars in the account for just this sort of thing.)

"Wha-cha-doin'?" Beth asked sleepily.

"Oh, sorry, I didn't mean to wake you."

"That's OK, I was just dozing. It's hard to sleep in the daytime." She yawned and stretched without opening her eyes. (Watching her, I felt like crawling back into bed.) "So, wha-cha-doin'?"

"Oh, just paying our moorage bill over at the Yacht Basin."

Pacific Gold

Her eyes popped open wide. "You're not going back there? What if Bully's still hanging around? What if he's got the cops watching for us?" She sat up, pulling the sheet defensively over her breasts.

"No, no, and no. Wouldn't think of it. I'm writing a check, and mailing it and the keys to the harbor master if I can find a mailbox or something close-by."

Beth let out a big sigh and settled back into bed. "Whew! sorry. Guess I don't want to get caught, we've just gotten started." She laughed. "That's a good idea. I should have thought of it last night."

"Hey, you did good last night. It wouldn't have worked if we had hung around any longer. I'm surprised Bully didn't fool around with that bar maid longer. No, I'd rather not see him any time soon either."

"He didn't sound pleased to be left behind on the dock."

"No, we'd better get some sea room soon. Time to get off this lee shore."

I launched the dinghy and paddled ashore. There was a gate-guard at the installation who promised to mail the envelope with the keys and money in it.

There was also a phone booth just outside the gate. I looked at it and thought, "Why not? I'll just check Bully's truth factor."

I dug our MCI card out of my wallet, (they wouldn't know that my address had fallen into the ocean.) I dialed about twenty five numbers and Uncle Milford said, "Good afternoon and may God bless you--**Today!**"

I said, "Hi Uncle Milford, this is Jack."

"Jack boy, how are you?" He paused slightly, but before I could comment he continued. "And more to the point, where in

Gawd's Great Green Creation are you? Did you and Beth really go over the cliff in that old house?"

"No, no, Beth and I are fine."

"Oh Lordy yes. I know'd the Creator'd be alookin' after you two. But that's been all the talk. There's been some people around lookin' for you'uns. There's talk that if you didn't go over the cliff with the house, you're in a heap of trouble with them environmentalists. Something about messing up the beach. I don't know how that could be. Act of Gawd. That's what I calls it. Ol' Lucifer's been alookin' to get that house since Great Grand Dad built it nigh unto a hunnert years ago. Yes sir, He set that ol' ocean a-gnawin' at that cliff just to bring it down. The Ocean giveth and the Ocean taketh away. She's Gawd A'Mighty's agent of vengeance here on earth. That's what I say, an I'll say it in any courtroom in the county. When you get ready to face the music, we'll be standing there with you."

"Well that's wonderful, Uncle," I broke in. I was getting nervous, so it might be true. Did I hear some extra clicks on the phone? Could Uncle's line be tapped by the Feds? And what about this military place over my shoulder? Some M.P. could come out the gate and grab me. (Paranoia strikes deep.) "Listen Uncle, I've got to go now--tell Aunt Hazel we are fine and we'll send a postcard when we can. And,...maybe it would be best if you didn't mention this phone call to anyone else,...OK?"

"What?...Oh sure, I understand." Uncle's voice dropped to a conspiratorial whisper. "OK then, take care now, and--we'll be a-prayin' for You!"

"Thanks Uncle. Bye-now."

I hung up and tried not to run back to the

beach. I tried not to row any harder than usual. I purposely stopped for five milliseconds to admire the bottom of the bridge. I still made it back to the boat in record time.

"So how'd it go? Find a mailbox?" Beth was sipping a cup of coffee in the cockpit.

"Yeah, no, the gate guard promised to mail it. There was a pay phone there too, so I gave Uncle Milford a call--what Bully said might be true." I climbed aboard Hispaniola.

"Really? So that's why you're so jumpy. You should have seen the way you were rowing."

"It was kind of hard to tell. You know how a conversation with Uncle Milford is. I might have jumped to conclusions, but..."

"But?"

"But it didn't sound good." I looked at the beach. The tide was returning. "Be a good time to sail," I commented. "The tides flooding, we could get out into the bay in time to ride the ebb out to sea."

Beth looked at me for a long moment and then said, "Well hey, it's Anchors Aweigh Time then. Let's hit the Briny Blue!"

Chapter 6: Two For The Briny Blue

• *2200, 20 October Crs: S.W.   Spd: 4 knts*
Dpth: O.S. Wx: Fog   Helmsman: Ishmael
Comments: Danger is a relative thing.

Up dinghy, up anchor, up sails--down the bay. A gentle west wind with small chop made for a nice beat into the late afternoon sunshine. A few sailboats were out, reaching and running about the bay, as well as a couple tugboats and freighters going about their business.

"Mmmm, I like this." Beth commented. She was lying on the lee side of the cockpit, out of the wind and in the sun, propped up by three boat cushions. "Let's just do this for awhile."

"OK." I agreed sleepily, I was sitting on the windward side, leaning against a back stay-- being kind of on watch--but mostly basking in the sunshine and feeling warm. To the west I could see the Golden Gate Bridge. Beyond that--

Pacific Gold

not so very far beyond--was the semi-permanent San Francisco fog bank. Knowing that it was waiting to welcome us back into its cold, damp embrace, made the sunshine even better. Of course, being the persistent optimist, I thought and hoped we'd be able to skirt it, at least for awhile--maybe we could just run south around it. It had to stop somewhere.

The tide turned when we were near Alcatraz. This gave us a nice push, but it also steepened up the choppy wind waves that the increasing wind pushed against us causing more spray to come over the bow. As the ebb's power built our speed over the bottom increased.

By the time we neared the Golden Gate bridge we were wide awake and in our foul weather jackets.

Suddenly Beth pointed and said, "Look! Up there on the bridge. There's someone up there!"

I casually looked up at the bridge. Of course there was someone up there, the place was crawling with people. I saw about a hundred cars crossing the bridge. Then I looked higher, up in the superstructure, thinking that she saw someone who was about to jump. "I don't see anyone besides about a hundred car drivers and passengers. Is someone going to jump?"

"No, no." Beth bounded through the hatchway, grabbed the binoculars, and stood in the companionway. "There. Right in the middle. Look! He's running our direction."

We were steering to pass under the bridge somewhat to the right of center. Now I could see a figure running along the bridge. "Oh, I see him. Do you think he's interested in us?"

"Here, you take a look." She handed the glasses to me. "*I* think it's Bully."

"What?" I tried to focus the binoculars. (I always have trouble with binoculars.) "Can't be." I found the running figure and managed, by closing one eye, and bringing the other into focus. "But it is. I can't believe it. What is he doing?"

"Well, it looks like he's trying to intercept us. He wouldn't jump off the bridge so we'd have to pick him up, would he?"

"Who knows? Anyone who would wait around on a bridge, for who knows how long, is capable of anything."

"We'll soon find out!"

It seemed as if we were being drawn towards the bridge at an alarming rate. I considered veering off north to avoid passing directly beneath Bully, but there was a tug and barge in that direction and I'd rather tangle with Bully than a tug and barge. I felt like a character in an Alfred Hitchcock movie being fatally sucked under the bridge to a rendezvous with destiny.

Destiny, as Bully orchestrated it, was soon revealed when he upended a case of beer bottles over the bridge-railing.

"Oh God. Look out!" Beth dove into the companionway and slammed the hatch to, over her head.

I, being at the helm as we entered the swirling waters between the bridge piers, had no choice but to remain at the tiller. I winced and flinched as the bottles smacked the boat. Fortunately the bottles were empty (or nearly so.) Most of the bottles shattered on impact, but one hit on the hatch, that Beth had just closed, bounced into the air landing at my feet in the cockpit well--unbroken.

As we slid under the bridge the decks were littered with broken glass and--*little slips of*

Pacific Gold

paper?

"What the hell? Beth...." I was about to ask her to grab one, but as we watched, they blew overboard.

"What was that all about? Notes in bottles?" Beth wondered out loud for both of us.

"Apparently."

"Boy, Bully should brush up on his interpersonal communication skills. I wonder what he had to say?"

"Well, here. Maybe there's something in this one?" I picked the one out of the cockpit and handed it to her.

Beth unscrewed the cap, which Bully had put back on after emptying the beer. She peered inside. "Yes, there's a slip of paper in there. It's kind of soggy though , and stuck to the side. I don't think Bully drank quite all the beer." She probed around with her little finger. "There...here it comes..." She carefully extracted what appeared to be a page from one of those little spiral bound notebooks that fit in a shirt pocket. After smoothing it on her thigh she said, "Hmmm, it's pretty smudged, I think he needs to sharpen his pencil, but it looks like a warning." She moved to get a better angle from the sun light and read, *"Stop! Go back! Trouble Ahead! Meet Me Sausalito S.B.H.!"* She looked up at me. "What's a S.B.H.?"

I was negotiating the last whirl pool before we sailed out from under the bridge. "Small Boat Harbor?" Overhead we could hear the honking of horns and squealing of tires. "Get ready, I think he's crossing the street. I hope he's out of bottles, but he may have something else."

We sailed free. "Look there he is!" Beth grabbed the field glasses. "Oh look, isn't that cute." she commented, the glasses to her eyes. "He's waving, with both hands...but he's only using one finger, on each." She waved back with all her fingers. "Bye bye Bully."

The rapidly ebbing tide against the strengthening sea breeze was setting up a steep chop. Hispaniola heeled to port and waves splashed over the bow washing broken glass out the scuppers.

"Now what?" Beth was still watching Bully through the binoculars.

I looked back and saw him running along the bridge.

"Is he going to Sausalito?"

"Wrong way."

He stopped at one of the girders. "Now what's he doing?"

"I can't tell for sure,....it looks like he is talking on a telephone. Maybe one of those emergency ones you see on bridges--or one of those that cops use? Is that possible?"

"With Bully, anything is possible." I turned my attention back to sailing. We were making great progress, even if it was getting bumpy. I could see that the fog bank was much closer than I had guessed. The wind was probably moving it in. It was already on the beach to the south. It was time to concentrate on sailing.

"Hey, what's with all these speed bumps? They're trying to make me seasick."

"You're sure it's not watching Bully that's making you sick?"

"Could be." She reached inside and put the binoculars in their slot. "What do you think he'll do next?"

I shrugged. "God only knows...."

"You mean Gwasasaee?"

"Is there another?"

As we moved farther out of the bay the wind veered more to the north, we eased the

Pacific Gold

sheets a bit and maintained our course close reaching westward. Our speed increased a bit more and the leeward rail stayed in the water.

"Do you think, maybe, we should put a reef in the main?" Beth suggested more than asked.

"Perhaps," I temporized as I peered ahead trying to determine whether the wind was strengthening or moderating farther out. It appeared that the wind was being funneled by the hills around the bay. Just then I heard the unmistakable whine of a Coast Guard helicopter. It appeared to be headed in our direction. "I think we should wait on that reef a bit." I pointed towards the helicopter. "I think I know who Bully was calling."

"That--son--of--a--bitch." Beth said slowly. The orange helicopter was speeding straight toward us now.

I looked at the fog bank ahead. I guessed that it was less than a mile away. If we were traveling at six knots, that meant that we could be in it in less than ten minutes. They would arrive in about thirty seconds. It would be a long ten minutes, but we might make it if they weren't too aggressive. I steered straight for the fog bank.

The helicopter swooped down and screamed past. I changed my mind. "I think we should take a reef or two. It won't slow us down. She might actually go faster on her feet, and if that helicopter, (which was turning to head back in our direction), starts hovering around us, it might be nice to have less sail up. And, it will look like we're doing something besides sailing straight for the nearest fog bank. I think *in* that fog bank would be a dandy place to be. We just might be able to lose them there. Would you please grab my sea boots, (I didn't want to step on any broken beer bottles in my bare feet on the fore-deck,) and then take the tiller?"

Beth disappeared into the cabin and reappeared with my yellow rubber boots. "Do you want socks?" she yelled over the scream of the helicopter as it came to a hover off the starboard side. Its rotorwash was buffeting us now.

I shook my head, "No," and reached to take the boots as she climbed out to take over the helm.

"Vessel Hispaniola!" A voice sounded over the meleé from the helicopter's P.A. system." This is the United States Coast Guard! Contact us on VHF channel sixteen immediately!"

I jerked on the boots and jumped up on the windward rail clutching a lower shroud. I waved my free arm and pointed to the main sail which was flopping around. Then I waved again, indicating that they should back off. With the added wind from their rotorwash the boat was on her ear but we were racing along at hull speed. Any delay would get us closer to the fog bank. They backed off a bit. I pulled myself forward to the main mast and loosened the halyard. "This should confuse them." I could have dropped it entirely, but decided to put the second reef in, it would take more time, and time was distance--and distance was what we needed.

The main was flapping wildly. The helicopter backed off further. I couldn't help smiling as I battled the big sail--slowly. On the other hand, I didn't want to get killed by the flailing boom. "Bring in the main sheet please," I yelled over the racket. "And keep heading for the fog--it's working!"

Beth held the tiller with her leg and hauled in the main sheet.

Pacific Gold

The boom steadied. I hooked the sail's tack on the reefing hook and tensioned the luff. The rotorwash from the helicopter pushed us along like a leaf in an autumn wind.

All that wind on the mizzen sail was giving Beth a workout on the tiller, but with her feet braced against the base of the mizzen mast, she was holding her own. Glancing forward I saw that the fog was even closer than I had hoped. With the helicopter's help we were flying along--so was the spray as we pounded into the chop, but who cared.

"Hispaniola! Come up on VHF, channel sixteen. Now!" The helicopter ordered.

I took the opportunity to suspend my reefing operations to jump to the rail and wave my arms like a crazy man again. I indicated the sail and waved for them to back-off. Amazingly, they did.

I turned and eased the mizzen sheet to give Beth some help. Wispy fogs were going by as I finished. "Almost there!"

"Hispaniola! You are going into the FOG! Turn back, NOW!! **You are standing into danger!! Return to PORT at ONCE!!!**"

I think the Helicopter Commander finally got the idea as we sailed into the obscuration. The helicopter approached rapidly from astern, but veered off at the edge of the fog bank while its rotorwash pushed us deeper into the gloom. We could still hear it overhead, but it was lost from view.

"Whew!" I collapsed into the cockpit beside Beth. "We did it." The wind was back to being a nor-westerly breeze. There was no spray in the air.

"Are we safe?"

"I think so." The helicopter seemed to be circling overhead. "I don't think that they can see any better in the fog than we can."

"What about radar?"

"Oh shit. Well, I can take care of that." I went forward to the flag halyard and lowered our radar reflector.

"OK, now we're a *stealth boat*. There are advantages to a wooden boat. We'll just have to keep a real good lookout."

"Great, just what I wanted to do. Keep a good lookout in the dark--in a fog bank. I guess it is better than going to jail for littering...is this what they meant by 'standing into danger?'"

"Right, I guess." I was suddenly very cold, and wet, and tired. I could use some dry clothes. I looked a Beth and she looked the same. "Well," I began with all the enthusiasm I could muster. "Why don't you let me take over the tiller while you get some dry clothes on?"

She looked over at me, "Good idea." She slowly released her grip from the tiller. "God, I'm exhausted. My hands are frozen." she marveled, rubbing and studying them in the dim light. "They're blue--and my nails are shot."

"I'm sorry, I'll buy you the best manicure in Tahiti when we get there with the treasure."

"It's a deal."

Pacific Gold

Chapter 7: The Briny Blue

-
- *0800, 25 October   Pos: N27°10' W126°38'*
Crs: South   Spd: 5 knts   Dpth: O.S.   Wx: Sunny,
puffy white clouds   Wnd: NNE @ 10 knts
Helmsman: Ishmael
Comments: Trade Winds!!

    Hispaniola passed Mile Rocks in the fog. (I could hear the horn bleating off the port side.) We held to our course of slightly south of west for another hour, then turned south--due south. I thought about doing evasive maneuvers, but decided they would be a waste of time since we could see nothing but cold, dark, gray, fog (besides, how evasive can you be at five miles an hour?)
    Leaving the companionway doors open, Beth worked on supper. "Do you think it'll be OK to turn on a galley light? They won't be able to see it will they?"

"I doubt it, and if they can--they're too damn close. I think that the only way they'll be able to find us in this fog is with infrared radar. I don't know if they have that in their helicopters."

"Well, even if they have it, it wouldn't have worked on me. I didn't have any detectable heat." She scratched a match and lit the galley lamp. "So, do you think we've gotten away?"

I was wondering that same thing, wondering if a submarine was about to pop up out of the fog and demand our surrender. "Yes, I think we've gotten away from the helicopter. But whether we've truly gotten away probably depends on how badly we're wanted. I think if they really want to stop us--they will. But then again, who knows? Certainly not me. Maybe satellites can detect wooden boats lost in the fog. Then again, how hard are they going to work to catch a couple of homeless litterers?"

So we sailed south in the fog, keeping four hour (or so) watches. Sometimes it was gray daylight and other times gray dark. We crossed major shipping lanes without seeing or hearing another vessel. The wind had stayed in the northwest and varied from ten to fifteen knots. Just right for a nice broad reach south.

"So what's the story here?" Beth asked at one of our watch changes. "I thought wind was supposed to blow fog away? Where's all this stuff coming from?"

"Beats me. The arctic, by the feel of it."

Beth shivered, "It's kind of like living in a wet towel. Where do you think we are?"

"Hard to say, but I suspect that we've passed the Mexican border and are somewhere west of Baja. I'd sure like to get some kind of a celestial sight soon."

Pacific Gold

"I could make out the moon for awhile, earlier. Should I have called you?"

"No, the sextant doesn't work without a horizon. It's a horizon that we need."

"Oh. Well, I haven't seen one of those for days. Nothing but this blessed wet fog. I don't know about you, but I think that we've been hidden long enough. I could use some sun today."

"Me too. I think a sweater is inappropriate wear for Mexican waters. Especially a damp sweater."

"God yes, everything's damp. I think I'm starting to mold."

It was four in the morning, or thereabouts. The swells were big, the wind had fallen off and shifted to the North. The main periodically blanketed the jib, then the jib rattled and banged on its track gybing and regybing. The vane was having trouble steering because the wind was so light, but also, I slowly realized, because of a smallish northeast swell. The little swell would pile up occasionally and gently thump the port quarter knocking the boat a little off course. I waited for it. It thumped the hull again.

"Did you feel that?"

"Feel what?" a note of concern sounded in Beth's voice.

"The cross-swell, from the northeast."

"Oh that. Yeah. It even slops over the rail a little occasionally.....why?"

"Well, if we just hang on a little longer-- I think this fog is going to clear."

"Oh. Well that's good news. Not really much else to do anyway--is there? Besides hang-on, I mean. It's not like we can walk home or anything, is it. I mean, we're *here!* Where-ever *here* is, until we get to someplace else. I mean--

oh shit, you know what I mean." Suddenly she was close to tears.

I put my arm around her shoulders and pulled her close, "Yeah, I know...." I almost said that I was sorry for dragging her out here to be cold and tired and wet and miserable, but I wasn't--and I didn't want to lie.

"I'm sorry," she mumbled. "I guess I'm just tired of this eternal dishrag fog." The little northeast swell thumped the hull hopefully. She sniffled. "So why do you think that new swell means the fog is going to clear out?"

"Well," I hesitated, not wanting to build up her hopes if I was wrong. "Well, the wind seems to be moving around to the north. Adding that to the northeast swell, I'd say we are getting close to the northeast trade winds--and trade winds don't have fog."

She considered that a moment. "Are you sure? Is this something you read in that book--Bowditch? Why wouldn't there be fog in the trade winds?"

"I think it's because ocean fog is formed by cold air passing over warmer water."

"Hmm, this is cold air alright."

"And the trades will be warm--straight from Baja--so, no fog."

"Hmmm, that sounds good." She sat up and looked around our very close horizon. It was a little after five a.m. and the fog was starting to be a lighter shade of gray. "It might be thinning a little," she said hopefully.

"Might be," I agreed, taking a deep breath. "Ahhh, I can smell tortillas on the wind."

"Rattle-rattle-bang." The jib completed a slam gybe to starboard.

"That's it. Let's gybe the main too and steer a little easterly. Maybe we'll intercept the

Pacific Gold

trades sooner. Anyway we'll be ready for them when they arrive." Actually, *we* would be the ones arriving. The Trades were where they were, but after days in the unchanging fog it seemed like we hadn't moved at all--lots of motion but no forward progress.

Amazingly my optimistic prediction came true. By ten o'clock we were sailing under sunny trade wind skies. The fog was just a damp memory that left a lot of wet clothes behind. But, as Beth said when we sailed out of it, "It served us well when we needed it--it just stayed around a little longer than necessary."

I missed the noon sight that had seemed so important in the fog. We were too busy enjoying the sunshine. I hauled out the sail bag of wet, salty, clothes that had been accumulating (and starting to smell bad) in the fore-peak. We rinsed them in a bucket of fresh water and hung them from the shrouds, booms, and life-lines to dry. That was so much fun that we decided to do the same for our damp, salty, bodies--which had also started to smell. Then lazing around in the sunny cockpit (drying), brought on the need for suntan lotion. And smearing that on each other felt so good that....well, the noon sight could wait for another noon.

We slept the afternoon away, together, for the first time since we were anchored at Treasure Island--so long ago and (I hoped) far away. After a delicious supper of fried potatoes with onions (fresh), corned beef (canned), corn (canned), wilted lettuce salad (the last of the it), and slightly moldy bread, I considered taking a round of twilight star sights. But, there was no land in sight and knowing exactly where we were just wasn't that important now. Besides, there were reasonably dry clothes to bring in.

The wind slacked with the sunset as we

sipped an after supper rum in a dry cockpit.

"Gosh, what a difference a sun makes." Beth commented.

"Mmmm," I agreed.

"It was important back on the Oregon coast, but not like at sea. Here it's essential."

"Mmmm yes." I was leaning back against the cabin bulkhead on the windward side, Beth was to leeward, we were both gazing over the stern towards Oregon. "Hard to believe that we've only been gone three weeks."

"Really? Is that all? Even San Francisco seems much longer ago than that. It seems dream-like now. Did they really chase us with a helicopter?"

"I don't know, I'll have to check the log book."

"I hope that it seems like a long time to them too."

"Like, maybe they've forgotten about us?"

"Yeah, that'd be nice."

"Especially Bully?"

"Jeez yes! Especially him!"

"You don't like him much?"

"Like him! Not in this lifetime."

"Pity. I think he was starting to appreciate your finer points."

"Ha! Like my bottom you mean. Did you see him try to pinch me? I should have slapped his face."

I chuckled, "Then he really would have thought you liked him."

"Hmmph!..........So, you and Bully go way back?"

"Almost all the way. Grade school, high school, until he quit. But I still saw him around until I joined the army and he joined the marines."

"You were buddies?"

"No, never that. But we had to co-exist, you know--interact? It was a small town."

"He was a marine? Hard to imagine."

"Briefly. He got kicked out or something. I don't know what happened. He was back home by the time I got to Nam."

"I'll bet he resents that."

"You think so? He always said he was too smart to go over there."

"Hey, you went to war and survived--he didn't. That's got to be hard on a tough guy's ego. Kind of like he missed out on a chance to prove himself?"

I shrugged my shoulders in the darkness, "Could be."

"It's funny how some people never seem to get it figured out. He probably envied you with your war hero Uncles, your family, your inherited social position. I'll bet he didn't have any of that."

"No, I don't suppose that he did. I think his family moved to town after he was born. They came from Oklahoma. His Dad was a log truck driver who drank too much and missed a turn on a mountain road. Bully was in high school when his Dad got crushed under a load of logs. He quit school and went to work in the woods to support his Mother and Sisters--but he didn't really. Support them much, I mean. Mostly he hung out in the bars with his woods buddies. His mom and sisters eventually moved back to Oklahoma, or someplace."

Beth yawned and stretched. "That's what I mean, it sounds like he couldn't help but make wrong choices."

"Kind of like, he was born to screw-up?"

"Something like that." The rum was gone, the wind down, the sea smooth, and the boat just rolling quietly along over the big swells under a starry sky. "Your watch?"

"Umm yeah." I sat up and glanced around the empty horizon. "Tired?"

"Always. I thought sailing was supposed to be easy?"

"Another myth exploded."

Beth yawned again. "Well I'm going to hit the sack." She said while climbing down the companionway steps carrying the empty rum cups.

"Looks like you've got your sea legs back."

"What? Oh yeah. I guess so. I don't notice the motion much any more." She rinsed and stowed the cups. "Need anything?"

"Just a kiss."

She gave me that and went forward into the dark cabin. I settled back enjoying the stars--for awhile. Then I got a craving for a cigar. I wished that I hadn't given up cigars. I realized it was good I did. OK--I really wished that cigars weren't bad for my health and that I had one to smoke *right now*.

"If wishes were fast trains..." OK, there's not a cigar within a hundred miles--I hope--so forget it. I know, I'll have a beer.

So I went down into the galley (quietly), found an amber ale, and returned to the cockpit. I pried off the top and took a long drink. Ahhhh, that's better.

My thoughts turned towards Bully. (It must have been the beer.) So was he predestined, as Beth suggested, to be a screw-up? Could be, whenever he was faced with a choice, he seemed to pick the wrong one--by my standards anyway. So what? I haven't always made the best of choices. Nam's a good example. I chose to join the army and go to Vietnam. Was that a good idea? Sure, I didn't know that the

Pacific Gold

people in charge were slime-ball politicians who didn't care about anything but their bank balances. I didn't know that we were supposed to fight and die for the economy--their economies. I signed up to fight a war like my Uncles. (When I stop to think about it, I guess they got the same raw deal.) Go out, kick ass, fight the Commies, and make the world a better place--the good old American way. But no, it turned out that the real enemy was running the government--*my* government. The enemy wore neckties, not black pajamas like they told us, politicians and lawyers. But I didn't know that then. Just another dumb kid from the sticks. But some people figured it out--maybe they made the right choice? Maybe it's not the choice, but the attitude? (It's the thought that counts?) And Bully? No, not Bully. He's just a misguided fuck-up. But if he made the right choice, Beth may be right, it was probably the wrong choice for him. Who can say?

    I guess I've always felt a bit sorry for Bully. Actually, if Beth hadn't of been there, or if we had a bigger boat, I might have taken him along at San Francisco. Now *that* would have been a bad choice. The truth is, I really can't stand him. I feel sorry for him, but I sure don't want to be stuck on a small boat with him.

    The ship's clock struck eight bells. Midnight already, time to wake Beth and let her commune with the stars.

    I woke Beth, and later Beth woke me. Actually she let me sleep a couple of extra hours before calling me to see the sunrise at six, in case I wanted to do some navigating.

    I took the hint and got a sight on Venus, the lower limb of the moon, and a bearing on the sun as it broke the horizon. I felt pretty proud of my accomplishment. And was even prouder an hour later when I made an X on the chart and announced to Beth, "Yes indeed, we are well out in the Briny Blue."

Pacific Gold

CHAPTER 8: The Good Life

- *1200, November 11 Pos: 0° N&S W127° 14'*
Crs: SSW Spd: 4 knts Dpth: O.S.
Wx: Sunny w/ small, puffy, white, clouds
Wnd: SSE @ 5 to 10 knts
Helmsman: Ishmael
Comments: Trade Winds!!

Beautiful sailing. Each day warmer than the one before. Warm winds, warm water, sunny skies, big smooth swells--the fabled northeast trade winds of the South Pacific Ocean.
There was, however, a small blot on the horizon when WWWV radio, in Hawaii, reported a tropical storm developing off the coast of southern Mexico. But it went north instead of west and the most we received from it was a cross swell from the east. By the time I was looking at the cross swell we were in relatively

safe waters south of all the projected storm tracks on the pilot chart.

Then we crossed the last regular shipping lane. Suddenly there was nothing to do but eat, sleep, cook, navigate, work on our tans, and sail the boat.

"So.....how do you know?" Beth asked when I told her that we'd crossed the last shipping lane. "We haven't seen a ship since we came out of the fog--or went into it again--for that matter. We could be the last two people on earth--or on ocean--or both."

"It says so here on the pilot chart," I explained from the navigation station (which happens to be the counter on top of the icebox.) "The last shipping lane runs from Balboa, Panama, to Honolulu, Hawaii. And by my noon sight, we are about fifty miles south of it."

"That's nice......I'd kind of like to see a ship though."

"That one we saw in the fog, north of San Francisco, was enough for me."

"Ugh. Don't remind me. I don't ever want to see one like that again...........no, I mean one off in the distance. You know, maybe two or three miles away," she said, pointing. "Maybe one over there, headed for Hawaii. Maybe a cruise ship, like the *Love Boat!*"

"I think the *Love Boat* is cruising in Alaskan waters these days."

"Phooey on that, I've had enough cold water sailing." She paused, gazing dreamily off towards the western horizon, "How about another sail boat then? Maybe someone like us. Another sail boat headed for French Polynesia? Or how about that Hawaiian boat!--Hokule`a?"

"Now that would be really neat, I'd love to meet her at sea." I looked west through the port hole, but the horizon remained empty. "Well, maybe later. But I wonder if she is out sailing about?"

Beth shrugged "...guess I'm just a little lonely."

"Yeah, it is kind of a big empty ocean isn't it." I paused and then remembered the good news that I had started out to tell her. "Anyway, I don't think we have to keep regular watches any more."

"No?"

"Without any ships to worry about, I think it'll be enough to just get up now and then, and have a look around. You know, make sure everything's OK. Make sure that the boat is still sailing in the right direction, check the horizon for squalls....."

"Sounds good to me. I could use a good nights sleep."

And, for the next four nights we did have nights of *better* sleep. But I don't think either of us got a lot of deep REM time. It was odd to wake up and realize that Beth wasn't out in the cockpit keeping an eye on things. Still, it was luxurious to lie in bed together most of the night.

On the fifth day we sailed into Hell. In the Sailing Directions (North Pacific), the area is referred to as the Inter-Tropical Convergence Zone or ITCZ, some people call it the Doldrums. Beth just refers to it as Hell.

As Navigator, I knew it was coming, of course. The Pilot Chart delineates it with wavy, dashed, blue lines. But the Sailing Directions say that it is highly variable and some times it's very narrow. I harbored hopes that would be the case in this case.

When Beth came below after an early morning look-around, she mentioned that there appeared to be a big cloud bank to the south.

"Oh," I said, my optimistic hopes dashed. "It's right on schedule then." I sat up in the bunk.

"What do you mean? Is there a storm forecast?"

"No, it's the Doldrums. If you'll bring the Pilot Chart over I'll show you."

She did, and I did.

She said, "Oh...so...we'll be becalmed?"

"I guess so, but I'm not sure." Pointing to the wind roses I went on. "You see? These indicate wind. So I don't know--maybe it'll just be a little squally." (My perpetual optimism.) "All the books say that the doldrums are unpleasant." I threw the chart over onto the table. "Anything else out there?"

"A couple of birds."

"Great." I lay back down and she slid under the sheet beside me.

"If it's going get bad ahead we'd better make the most of this nice sailing." she murmured in my ear.

I concurred.

We entered Hell somewhat later. I was below working out the noon sight. The trade wind had mostly fizzled out, and it looked as if we really might get becalmed. I heard the sails flapping and Beth say, "...winds shifted to the southeast." The sheet winch clicked as she sheeted in the jib, then the blocks squeaked and creaked as she pulled in the main and mizzen booms. "We're close hauled," she commented. The boat heeled to starboard.

"It could be the S.E. trades," I commented hopefully, and went on with my calculations.

The sails flapped and slammed across to port. "Good grief! Now the winds southwest," Beth reported from the cockpit.

"Not the S.E. trades," I said. I tried to keep

Pacific Gold

my books and calculations on the table as the boat heeled to port. We hadn't been on this tack for ten days, consequently everything that had settled to the starboard side had to shift over to port. Pots, pans, cans of food, pillows, books, and everything else that had space to move--did.

The sea was becoming lumpy too. As I chased my pencil across the cabin sole, I realized that completing my calculations could wait for a better time. I scurried about stowing things as Hispaniola became increasingly active.

"Shit! The winds dead ahead--and we're dead in the water! What should I do?.......Jack?............*Jack??*"

Below, I was battling chaos. Stuff came out of everywhere as the boat rolled from rail to rail. Suddenly, I had to get out. I fought my way to the companionway and climbed shakily out the hatch.

"Watch your head!" Beth cried out as the boom swung across and all the sails flapped. "You alright?"

I tried, briefly, to figure out which was the lee rail--couldn't--headed for the one that was down--it was up by the time I reached it--it didn't matter. I sacrificed my lunch (and quite possibly some breakfast) to Neptune. After rinsing my face with some handy sea water, I felt better.

By then the boat had fallen off the wind and Beth was steering to keep the wind in the sails in an attempt to steady the boat.

I hauled myself back by the tiller, across from Beth, and wedged myself into the corner of the cockpit. The sky was overcast, the temperature had to be about a hundred degrees, Hispaniola was pointed towards Guatemala, and it started to rain.

"Jeez! I guess we've arrived in the Inter-

Tropical Convergence Zone," I commented, and timed a lunge with the boats roll to pull the hatch shut.

"I think we've just reached Hell. Those old-time sailors who said that if you sailed too far you'd go over the edge were right!....I don't suppose that there is any turning back?"

(Now there was an appealing thought.) "No--it would just prolong it. Once you get to Hell you've got to go on through." Hoping for inspiration, I studied the situation. The wind was too light to keep the sails filled when we rolled, so the booms flopped and the sails popped dumping what little wind they did manage to catch. The noise was incredible. It was a major effort to just hold on while the boat sharply pitched and rolled at random. Meanwhile we slowly sailed in the wrong direction.

Tightening the sheets helped a little, at least it limited the travel of the booms as they flopped. "Can you steer towards the south at all?" I asked trying to be tactful.

"Here, you take the tiller and see what you can do? I'll try to restore some order below."

I took over the helm. This was hard core sailing. I had two goals--keep the boat moving and keep heading south.

Beth did a masterful job of controlling the chaos below. She even managed a peanut butter and honey on pilot bread sandwich, to replace the lunch I had given to the sea. The noise reduction she managed helped a lot, but the banging and popping of the sails was nearly intolerable. I was sure something was going to break with every roll. But, eventually, I became reconciled to it. If something was going to break--it would. All we could do was to keep sailing south, the faster we went south, the sooner we'd get out of this mess.

Pacific Gold

We took turns, trying to sail, trying to sleep, trying to cook. By the third day it was simply survival. I was at the helm at 0900. We were making about two southish knots in hazy, humid, sunshine. Beth was putting away the cereal bowls from breakfast. I glanced up at the main, just in time to see it start to split.

"Beth! Come take the tiller!"

"What?"

"Come take the tiller! Quick!" I watched as the boat rolled again and the belly of the sail ripped open. "Shit."

Beth climbed into the cockpit. "What's the rush?"

I pointed to the sail. "I guess the rush is over."

"Oh my." Beth stared in awe at the giant gap.

I too stared at the rip. "I guess we'd better get it down and start sewing."

"Oh." Beth slid back beside the tiller. "Guess I should have been quicker, huh? Sorry."

I shrugged. "It wouldn't have made any difference. I don't think we could've stopped it anyway."

I sheeted the boom in tight, tensioned the topping lift, and dropped the remains of the big sail. It was ripped clear across only being held together by the bolt rope and leech line. I considered trying to sew it on the boom, but the boat was rolling even more with out the resistance of the main sail. Just staying on the cabin roof was a major effort. The thought of trying to sew in the rolling cabin made my stomach queasy. This was not going to be fun.

I temporized by stuffing most of the big sail into the forward end of the cockpit well with part of the rip up. Beth graciously volunteered to start sewing if I would take over the helm. I quickly accepted her offer and retreated to the tiller.

Beth found the sewing stuff, cut some long patches from spare sail cloth and set to work with needle and palm. Holding the three pieces of cloth positioned correctly and sewing was nearly impossible on the rolling boat, but she persevered. She made a half dozen stitches and studied her work. "It's not going to be very pretty," she observed.

"That doesn't matter, just so it holds."

"If there was some way to clamp the pieces together it would sure help. If the damn things would just stay put!" she muttered as she made a grab for the sail-twine that was trying to get away.

I had let the boat come up too close to the wind, the jib slatted and the boat rolled extra far. I pulled back off the wind a bit.

"Could we glue it?" Beth asked.

"Hmmm, I think gluing would be tough. But...how about...Duct Tape?"

"Would that work?"

"We could tape the thing together on one side and sew the patch on the other."

"You mean, just sew through the tape?"

"Yeah, I guess so. Wouldn't hurt anything."

"Well OK, let's give it a try. It should make a distinctive looking sail."

"Sure, one silver stripe. If we like it we can do the other sails to match."

"Let's not get carried away."

So we taped and sewed and rolled and cussed and sweated and stabbed our fingers with needles and cut our hands with sail-twine; until we were both cross-eyed, queasy stomached, and ready to walk home. But at noon the next day we held our breaths as the sail went aloft.

Pacific Gold

The patch held!

The boat still rolled, the sails still slatted, our progress was still minimal; but it was so much better with the sail back up that life seemed almost tolerable.

That night, I was fighting to stay awake as the tiller alternately tried to jerk my arms off and jab me in the ribs. The evening squalls had passed and we were mostly becalmed. Hispaniola spun in slow circles. Every time I looked at the compass we were pointed a different direction. The boat slopped about randomly this way and that with no discernible rhythm or pattern. I hurt. I was exhausted. My eyes wouldn't stay open and the boat wouldn't let me sleep. My fingers were sore and swollen from cuts and salt water. I was damp, cold, salt encrusted. If I wasn't so tired I might have been hungry too. I felt like a used punching bag with half its stuffing gone, the kind you see kicked into a corner at the oldest, nastiest, dirtiest, thrift-stores.

Suddenly the boat took a giant roll, scooping up water with both rails. The tiller jerked out of my hand and slammed against the port cockpit combing, then came back whacking me in the ribs, it slammed against the combing again, then it was back among my ribs.

"Arrrgh!!" I was suddenly wide awake and angry. Grabbing the tiller with both hands I subdued it, wrapped the end of the main sheet around it, and tied it down. I hauled in the sheets until all the sails were as tight as I could make them. "There damn-it-all, go were you will!" I told Hispaniola with quiet ferocity, and went below. I wedged myself into a corner behind the table and surrendered to fatigue.

When I became conscious again, the sun was shining through the port-holes, the sails were rattling, and the boat gently rocked from side to side. It took me a few moments to realize that the sails weren't slatting, and we weren't pitching and rolling erratically. It was *peaceful*.

I carefully extracted myself from the settee corner. I hurt. My body was a wreck but my mind was jubilant--it was a beautiful day! I turned to the bunk where Beth lay secured by lee-cloths. Her hair was matted and stringy with salt, she had a big bruise on her forearm, her fingers were covered with cuts and band-aids, but she was softly snoring with the face of a child.

I stumbled quietly on deck. Hispaniola was sailing herself into a light south-east breeze and a small regular swell.

We'd made it. We had paid our price to Neptune and regained paradise.

Slowly I untied the tiller, cracked the sheets and trimmed the sails for a close reach on the port tack to sail South.

South on the South East Trade Winds!

CHAPTER 9: LANDFALL

- *2200, November 19, At Anchor--Taa Huku Bay, Hiva Oa, Marquesas Islands, French Polynesia-- Beautiful, well protected bay, two fathoms, good holding ground.*

On we sailed, south-south-west; broad reaching on the south east trades. The trades were actually blowing more east than south. Couldn't ask for better. Beautiful day after beautiful day--hot though, very hot. "Hotter than seven barrels of owl poop," as the old man used to say. Beth said it was the first time she was someplace where she could break a sweat naked, and doing nothing.

Each afternoon, after figuring the noon sight, I extended the line on the chart a little farther. I had just finished plotting a new position when Beth descended languidly into the galley.

"Do you want to split the last apple?" she asked. "I don't think that it will keep much longer." She held up a shriveled little thing that would never have tempted Adam, but it looked pretty good to me.

"Sure, let's finish it up. A couple more days and we'll be eating fresh mangoes."

Beth was busy precisely dissecting the apple, but she stopped with the knife half through it. "What do you mean?"

"Well, by my calculations--with any luck at all--some time the day after tomorrow--or so--we should be dropping the old hook into Polynesian sand."

"Really?"

"Honest Italian." Putting my right hand over my heart I raised my left.

"You're not Italian and I'm from Missouri--show me." She looked eagerly at the chart.

"OK. We're about here." I said, pointing to the "x" marking my noon sight. "And here...is Hiva Oa. It's about 200 miles away...sooo, at a hundred miles a day...it looks a lot like noon, day after tomorrow!"

She stared at the chart. First at the short distance to the islands and then at the long, long, distance we'd come. "Wow, it's unbelievable." She glanced up at me and back to the chart. "I mean I always thought that we'd make it, but golly--it looked so far--and--and it's been so long--and--and suddenly--here we are!!" She hugged me joyously. "We're really here....in the *South Seas!*"

We ate the shriveled up apple looking at the chart. Later, while we were relaxing in the afternoon shade of the mainsail a new bird flew by.

"Frigate Bird!" we exclaimed simultaneously, pointing and laughing. The big black and white bird cut a lazy circle above the boat, then wandered off--southeastward.

"I guess one of us isn't headed for the nearest land," I remarked.

"Naw, it's too early. She's still grocery shopping," Beth replied confidently.

I looked at her with raised eyebrows.

"Hey, don't give me that. I've read about it in *my* books. Just like Noah, the birds showed the Ancient Polynesians where land is."

I thought about that a moment. "Maybe he'll be back later to show us the way?"

"I'll bet she is," she said very definitely.

"What'll you bet?"

"Ooooh." She grinned mischievously. "No." Then, "I know. If she comes back by on her way home you cook supper. If she doesn't, I will."

We shook on it.

Later, as I was cooking the macaroni, I didn't think the birds would ever quit coming by.

"Here come three more!" Beth yelled jubilantly down the hatchway. "Yessir, makin' a bee-line for their little island home."

"So, are you sure that the same one has gone by?"

"Absolutely!"

"Are they going the same way we're going?"

"Hmmm, maybe a point or two starboard, Capt'n."

"Good, that means they're headed for Fatu Huku and we're not."

Beth looked down the companionway into the galley from the hatch cover on which she was lying. Her was face upside down and her sun bleached hair hung below it like Spanish Moss. "Headed for a fat what?"

"Fatu Huku. It's the closest island. We

have to pass it to get to the port of entry, Atu Ona, on Hiva Oa."

"Can't stop, huh?"

"Not legally."

"OK. Let's not. I've had enough of that cops and robbers stuff."

"Right-o Matey." I looked up from my cooking but her face was gone.

I heard her mutter indistinctly "So what is a fat huku?"

When I stepped up the companionway to announce dinner she was lying on her back on the hatch cover. I saw a tangle of hair, the silhouette of her nose neatly bisected the twin silhouettes of her breasts against the sunset orange mainsail. I paused, savoring the image, but she heard my sigh and rolled over onto her side. "Supper ready Capt'n?"

"You bet, ships blue plate special; macaroni and cheese, creamed corn, and corned beef on the side...again."

"Mmmm, sounds delicsh. I'm starved."

And a little later, after most of my culinary creation had been consumed, she commented, "Just think--two days from now we'll be eating roast pig and drinking rum under the palm trees."

And later, when we were lying in bed being gently rocked by the sea, she said, "You know, I don't think I've ever seen a real palm tree, I mean outside of a mall or post-card."

I squeezed her hand, "You won't be able to say that after the day after tomorrow."

"No...D'ya know what I'd really like to do?" she asked sleepily. "I'd like to make love.......in the sand....under a palm tree........."

"Mmmmm........me too.........let's."

"Mmmmm...."

The next day there were more birds. We

studied them and the horizon too, even though we knew we shouldn't be able to see anything yet. The noon sight confirmed that we were still about sixty-three nautical miles from Fatu Huku--too far to see it. But still--we looked forward and our thoughts went with the birds as they flew home.

At supper time we took our supper, (corned beef, boiled potatoes, and creamed corn,) forward to eat it on the foredeck. There we had an unobstructed view, under the genny, towards the islands. We saw tons of birds, but no islands. There were some mighty stationary clouds, but no islands. The trade winds faltered with the setting of the sun, but didn't die. Hispaniola gently sailed herself onward. We sipped the last of our California wine as twilight faded and the stars brightened.

"So it's tomorrow then?"

I lifted my cup from my belly and turned on my side to face Beth's silhouette. "Tomorrow. Unless my navigation is totally off--and the birds are a collective illusion that we've dreamed up."

Beth sighed a long dreamy sigh, "No, the birds are real. I trust the birds."

"And my navigation?"

She turned onto her side to face me. She carefully placed her wine cup at the foot of the mast, then put her arm around me and her lips brushed mine as she said, "Your navigation is good, very good. I trust your navigation..."

Later, as we made out way below to turn in for the night, she said, "You know, in a way, I feel sorry that we are going to make landfall tomorrow. I mean, this has been kind of wonderful--kind of magic. Just the two of us and all that. Kind of like time out, and tomorrow we'll be back in the game again."

"Yes, a different game, but still...," I ran out of words and then said, "Time out is nice. I like time out a lot. Let's do it again?"

"Yes. After we find the Treasure."

"Ah, the Treasure. I'd almost forgotten."

In truth we hadn't mentioned the Treasure for days, before the equator and the doldrums. It had slipped to the back of my mind. "Yes, it is definitely back in the game we'll be-- the Treasure game!" I said, warming to the idea. "We're getting closer, Love."

"Mmmm, very closer," she said, as she snuggled against me.

And then a little later, "It'll sure be nice to have clean sheets again."

The clock was striking four bells and its hands pointed to six. The trade wind was puffing gently through the open port-hole along with the bright morning rays of sunshine when Beth slipped quietly out of bed.

She was barely out the hatch when she announced, **"Land Ho!! Ho! Ho! Ho!"** Beth's glowing face appeared in hatchway. "Hey! Get out of bed you Lazy Lubber! Thar's land off the starboard bow!"

I considered pretending nonchalance, but it was too late--I was already up the companionway steps. Outside there was a giant rock in the water a few miles off the starboard bow.

"Fatu Huku?" Beth asked.

"Must be." As I stared, long skeins of birds were trailing off the rock; seaward. It was a beautiful rock, all brown and green in the morning sunlight. Or was I imagining the green? Such an incredibly beautiful green. Polynesia! We had made it. Incredible. I suddenly realized that, on some level, I had doubted that we ever really would be here. Entranced, I stared as I peed over the side. (I peed on my foot too. But no problem, a quick rinse in the ocean put it right.)

Noticing, (as she stood naked on the bowsprit,) Beth said, "I'm not sure you're ready for civilization."

"I'll bet they're used to sailors."

A couple of hours later we saw Mount Ootua materialize from a cloud. As the day progressed Hiva Oa slowly emerged from the sea.

Another magical day. We ate, bathed in the cockpit, cleaned the boat; through it all we looked, and looked, and looked at the growing island off the bow. It changed from a distant gray-green into vibrant tropical green, underlined by brilliant white surf crashing on the shiny black rocks of Cape Balguerie and Motu Tapu.

We had long since run out of superlatives by the time we eased past the Cape for a leisurely down wind run along the south shore. That was when the island's perfume reached out to us.

"Wow!"

There was nothing else to say. Entranced by the presence of the island, we didn't notice the macaroni and cheese we mechanically consumed for lunch.

Finally, as the sun set, we ghosted into Taa Huku Bay and dropped our anchor on Polynesian sand. After furling the sails, we sat in the cockpit trying to take it all in.

"Will the authorities mind if we don't go ashore until until morning?"

In the distance we could hear voices mingled with lapping wave sounds. A rooster crowed. The air was laden with a smoky perfume.

"Does it matter?" I asked, turning to her in the twilight.

I saw her slow smile. "No," she said, nodding her head in agreement. She reached out and touched my arm. "Jack, I just want you to know, whatever happens, this is worth it."

Even though it had been a long, exciting day, we did not go to sleep immediately. We lay snuggled in the bunk listening to the distant night sounds. Island sounds, and the occasional sound of little wavelets lapping against Hispaniola's hull.

"Jack?"

"Mmph," I replied into her hair.

"It's so quiet and still. It's almost too peaceful."

"Mmmm....Hispaniola sleeps."

"Yes. *The Good Ship Hispaniola.* She carried us all the way; through storm and fog and sea without complaint.

"Through Hell."

"Hmm yes...through Hell." A sleepy chuckle. "She hasn't slept since San Francisco...."

"Dozed a couple of times, but never really slept."

"She sleeps now...." Then Beth slept.

And Jack too.

CHAPTER 10: ATU ONA

Awake at four bells. Beth has already slipped from the bunk. A rooster crows somewhere in the distance. The air is almost cool. The boat, motionless, still sleeps after her long, pitching, rolling, bouncing journey south.

Topside, I found Beth reclining in the morning sunshine on the port side (her favorite side) of the cockpit. Her long tee shirt reminded me that we are among people again. I grabbed a towel to wrap around me before stepping into the sunshine.

"Bonjour, mon Capitaine."

"Ah...Oui...Bonjour Madame Mate."

She stretched and waved our French-English dictionary. "I've been studying--a little. Ooh, it's sooo deliciously nice." She waved her arms indicating the whole bay (maybe the world.) "I took a swim."

"How was it?"

"Best ever."

"Hmmm." I glanced around the bay, saw no one, stepped to the more private side (starboard), dropped my towel and stepped over the rail. Splashing deep into the deliciously warm salt water, I surfaced and paddled around the boat.

"Well?" Beth asked when I got to the port side.

"Best ever." I agreed. "Got any soap?"

"Sure." She tossed the plastic bottle of dish soap in my direction.

After breakfast we launched the dinghy and rowed to the beachward. Hand and hand we crossed the white sand on rolling sea legs and stepped into a small enchanted grove of coconut palms. It was green, green, green. Grass, ferns, creepers, bushes; here and there were unbelievably bright colored blossoms. And the smells! After weeks of sensory deprivation at sea, even the smoke from a smoldering pile of old coconut husks smelled good.

We reached the red dirt road that led to the village of Atu Ona. Suddenly, it was incredibly hot. "I don't want to complain, but what happened to the Trade Winds?"

We were hiking up hill and, stopping for a breather, we could see the "Big Ocean" outside the bay. "There they are." I said, pointing seaward.

We were still admiring the view when an old flat-bed pick-up chugged up the road and stopped. It was loaded with women and kids who all said, *"Bonjour.*(plus a lot of other things we didn't understand.)"

We said, *"Bonjour, Bonjour,"* and climbed on board.

As we bumped slowly along the dusty red dirt road a large matron, dressed in *pareu* and giant brassiere, with a small child and a piglet resting comfortably on her spacious lap, engaged Beth in friendly conversation punctuated with big smiles. We couldn't understand much of what she said but the meaning was clear. "The natives are friendly."

The overloaded truck swayed and rocked into the little village of Atu Ona. The flowers and trees along the street perfumed the humid air. We all piled off when the truck stopped in front of a store. Several people pointed down a side street saying, *"Gendarmerie."*

"Merci, merci beaucoup. Au revoir."

We set off towards a small building with a French tricolor flag out front. Inside we discovered a large Polynesian sitting behind a battered desk scowling at a document lying on it. His uniform shirt and cap were faded but neat and clean.

"Bonjour Monsieur," I said timidly.

Startled, he jumped to his feet with a big smile, *"Bonjour, Bonjour!!!."*

Easily the largest man I have ever seen engulfed my hand in his and shook it. He turned to Beth, briefly took her hand and indicated a chair, *"Madame."*

Beth sat, and at his direction I also sat. He returned to the chair on the other side of the battered desk. Brushing the troubling document aside he inquired with an encouraging smile, *"Comment ally vous?"*.

I handed him our passports.

"Ahhhh," he said appreciatively. Opening them carefully with his banana sized fingers, he looked from the photos to our faces and back again. *"Bon."* He declared, and turned the pages to our visas. Again he smiled and said, *"Bon."*

He shuffled through the rest of our

papers; the boat documents and crew list. Finally he picked up a big rubber stamp and, with obvious satisfaction, slapped it down repeatedly on the papers.

While doing this he knocked the paper that he had been studying, when we interrupted, off his desk. It sailed to the floor near my chair. I leaned over and picked it up. The words, "URGENT COMMUNIQUE and U.S. Coast Guard", leaped out at me. I scanned the rest of it as casually as I could while returning it to the desk.

The *Gendarme* jumped to his feet and came around his desk saying, "Welcome to *Polonaise Français!*" *"Monsieur."* He handed me the boat papers and shook my hand. Turning to Beth he said, *"Madame."* He gently grasped her shoulders and quickly kissed both her cheeks.

We stumbled out onto the dusty street and into the brilliant mid-day sun. With the exception of a couple of dogs and a pig sleeping under a big mango tree, the village appeared to be deserted. "Gee, where did everyone go?"

"Beats me, let's go to the store. Maybe we can get a cold beer."

The store was empty with exception of a little old Chinese Man sleeping on the counter by the cash register. He sat up and yawned when we came in. *"La sieste."* he said, either as explanation or reprimand.

"Hinano?" I asked.

He sleepily indicated a cooler.

I took out an ice cold liter of beer. Beth opened another cooler and found a half liter of ice cream.

Rather than trying to communicate verbally the shopkeeper scribbled the price on a scrap of paper. I paid and he put the money on the cash register with an automatic, *"Merci."*

"Merci beaucoup." We headed for the door as he stretched out on the counter again.

We found an unoccupied shady spot under a convenient mango tree to consume our ice cream and beer.

"All right, so what did that paper you picked up off the floor say?" Beth asked.

I looked at her with a questioning expression.

"Come on, I saw your face when you read it and it didn't look good."

"OK. It was from the Coast Guard asking for information on a yacht named Hispaniola."

"Hmmmm...so what does that mean?"

"Good question. I guess that it could mean anything. At the very least it means that someone *is* interested in us."

"Just who that someone is, that's the question of the day."

"I guess the *Gendarme* didn't catch it, I wonder if he reads english. Maybe he'll forget about that aggravating message from the United States."

"I hope so."

"Me too."

Beth leaned back against the tree and sighed. "It sure is nice here. But I guess this means that we'll be shoving off soon."

I shrugged my shoulders, "Perhaps.....I'm really curious about exactly *who* is looking for us. Is it really the E.P.A., or is it just Bully posing as a concerned citizen or something?"

"I don't know which would be worse." Beth commented.

The beer tasted good and the warm fragrant breezes were marvelous. A severe case of mellowing-out was in progress. It was hard to believe that anything bad could happen in such a peaceful, pleasant place. There was a familiar quality to this feeling--a deja vu sort of a thing.

Then I remembered. This was the way it was in Vietnam Nam. Sometimes everything got quiet and I could sit back with a beer and admire the beauty and peacefulness of the place. Until a rocket or mortar round or something turned the whole thing back into chaotic reality.

I tried to shrug off the desire to just forget it and kick back. But if we waited around, I felt sure a bomb would drop. "Well shit, maybe we'll find out someday. Someday after we find the treasure. Until then I think that we ought to avoid unnecessary confrontation with officialdom."

"Which means, shoving off."

"Yeah."

"Don't we have to tell the *Gendarme* before we leave?"

I nodded.

"Won't he be suspicious? I mean, we just got here after a month at sea."

"Hmm, that's true. We don't want to out smart ourselves. Maybe we should hang around for a day or two before heading for the Tuamotus." My gut feeling still was to run, but, maybe it would be better to hit the dirt instead, lie low for a couple of days. Gut feelings are over-rated anyway. My gut was full of a dubious combination of ice-cream and beer--with a touch of fear thrown in. Not the most reliable of prophets.

We lounged under the mango tree until people started reappearing, and then went back into the store. The shop keeper was up and about, almost congenial. Beth learned that *la sieste* was from noon to two, also that fresh French bread was to be found at the baker's house, and that fresh fruit could be obtained

Pacific Gold

from anyone who had some.

We went to the baker's. His wife let us buy two loaves and told us that if we wanted more, we'd have to order it for the next day. She said that they had baked these two extras because our boat was reported to them the night before. (We ordered four loaves.)

When asked about fresh fruit the baker's wife, summoned a small boy who took us to another house. There a very skinny old man supplied us bananas, papayas, all the mangoes we could carry, and a pomplemoose. He said something about "Yankees", called me "Joe", said something else about the French, spat vehemently in the dirt, patted me on the back, and refused my money.

With our back packs full, we headed back to the boat. All in all it had been a very nice day, with the exception of the nagging feeling that we were about to be imprisoned. Oh well, every rose bush has its thorns.

It was easy to laze away an additional two or, actually, three days in that idyllic bay. It seemed too soon when I made my way back to the *Gendarmerie.* I had an unreasonable fear of not coming out a free man.

Consequently I had a beer at the store before timidly approaching the large Gendarme behind the rickety desk.

"*Bonjour Monsieur,*" he greeted me when I entered his office.

"*Bonjour Monsieur,*" I hesitantly responded, wishing Beth were there to speak French for me.

I gave it up and tried English. "Ah, we would like to sail on to the Tuamotus.".

He gazed at me for a moment before responding. "So soon? The Tuamotus. Very good. Are you going to visit any other islands in the Marquesas?"

"You speak English," I blurted out in surprise.

"But of course. I live one time in Los Angeles."

"Why didn't you speak English the other day when we first came in."

The big man shrugged his shoulders gesturing with huge hands. "Sailboat people come from the U.S., they expect to speak French here--I don't like to disappoint them." He shrugged again and smiled.

"So, it's the Tuamotus, is it?"

"Yes. It would be nice to visit more of the Marquesas Islands though. This is a beautiful place."

"A lot of the cruiser's go South from here to Tahu Ata, and on to Fatu Hiva before going further West. Once you leave the Marquesas--it is hard to come back against the wind."

"Could we do that without returning to Hiva Oa?"

He gazed speculatively at me and finally replied, "*Oui,* I could stamp your *passeport* now, and clear you on to the Tuamotus. You must check in with the resident *Gendarme* at each island, but you must have my stamp to leave the Marquesas."

"I'd like to do that. Fatu Hiva, isn't that where Thor Heyerdahl tried to live back before World War II?"

"Ah, you know of him." he laughed. "Yes, he tried to go native--but without understanding what that meant. That is big mistake of Europeans. Paul Gauguin, he is buried here, had the same problem. (Did you visit his Grave? It's just up the hill in the cemetery.) He didn't respect his own people, or ours either--miserable man."

I thought of the books I had read about the South Sea Islands. All written by foreigners. I wondered what the Polynesian version of the story would be? What did they think about all the white seafarers who changed their way of life? Have they written any books?

"Americans do better." The big man interrupted my thoughts, "There was one my father used to talk about, Jimmy Hall. He was a writer. Not, I think, a very successful one--but he was happy."

"James Norman Hall? I've read his books. I think he was a very good writer. One of my favorites. Though, as you say, he was probably not as successful as some. He is very good. And, as you say, I think that he was happy."

"Ah yes. *Bon!*" He opened a desk drawer and extracted our passports. Opening them he made some notations with a ball point pen, then pensively stamped them. He closed them and carefully stacked one on top of the other, keeping his big hand on them.

"A curious co-incidence. Just before you arrive I receive a request from the U.S. Coast Guard for information about a yacht with same name as yours, Hispaniola. But I think it was referring to a larger vessel. Are you aware of any other boats with the same name?"

"No, but I suppose there might be others. It seems like there are more boats then there are boat-names."

"Ah yes, this is true. One year four, Dawn Treaders, passed through. I think they got the name from some book."

"We got the name *Hispaniola* from a book-- *Treasure Island*, by Robert Louis Stevenson."

"Yes, that's it! I read this book! I thought the name familiar. I couldn't think where. *Merci, merci beaucoup!* Thank you for solving the puzzle." He pushed the passports across the desk and shook my hand. "You must be going."

"*Oui,*" I said as he released my hand and the passports. *"Merci, merci beaucoup Monsieur!"* I headed for the door.

"*Capitaine,*" I stopped in the door. "If perhaps, you should encounter another vessel of that name?--tell them that the U.S.Coast Guard would like to speak with them, eh? I personally have no use for your Coast Guard--too pushy--but..." another Gaelic shrug.

"Ah, do you know what the Coast Guard might want to speak with them about?"

"   *Non,* is probably trivial." Another shrug. "*Bon!*" He clapped his hands. *"Bon voyage!"*

"*Au revoir Monsieur!*"

As I started towards Taa Huku Bay an airplane passed over head. I happened to be passing the store, so I asked the men lounging on the front stoop. *"Quest-ce que c'est aeroplane?"*

"*Oui, aeroplane,*" they agreed, nodding their heads.

"Ah...*de jour?*"

"*Es lundi.*"

"Ah....*aeroplane arrivé lundi?*"

Vigorous nodding. *"Oui, lundi."*

"Aussi mardi?"

"*Non, non,*" Vigorous head shaking and laughter. *"Lundi! Lundi spécifique! Air Polonaise Lundi seulement!"* they shouted.

"Ahhh, Oui, Oui, Tre Bien! Air Polonaise--Lundi. Merci beaucoup."

They were all smiles now, they had gotten through to the dumb foreigner. I shook their hands and bid them *"Au revoir."*

I walked on. It was nice to know that even here people spoke more forcefully when someone didn't understand the language. It was also nice to know that if a person wished to fly in or out,

Pacific Gold

he could do it on a Monday. Presumably there would also be, at least, weekly air service to some island in the Tuamotus.

I was still pleased with myself for acquiring that bit of knowledge as I approached the coconut grove that hid the beach where the dinghy waited. What a beautiful day. I had walked all the way from the village and wasn't too uncomfortably hot. I must be getting acclimated to the tropics.

Strolling down the last bit of red dirt road I idly watched a truck approaching from the other direction. It was trailing a large plume of dust. As it passed me I waved to the crowd of people in the back and found myself looking straight into the sweating red face of a large man wearing a very colorful Hawaiian shirt and a dirty, "Cat", ball cap. Bully!

"**Jackeeee!!**" he stood up and yelled gleefully.

"Oh God! Oh God oh God oh God oh God," The bomb had just *arriveéd* on the weekly *aeroplane.*

God took pity on the dumb Sailor who should have sailed yesterday. As the truck sped on down the road through the cloud of dust I saw Bully waving his arms, wildly gesturing. For a moment I thought he might jump or fall off, but he didn't and the truck kept on going over the hill.

I stepped into the coconut grove and ran for the dinghy. "...and run for the harbor, that's the life of a Sailor man--again!"

Chapter 11: Anchors Aweigh--Again!

• *0700 23 November Pos: SW of Hiva Oa*
Crs: 240° Spd: 3 knts Dpth: O.S.
Wx: light trade winds, sunshine, Purrfect!(Beth)
Helmsman: R.L.S.
Comments: Hot on the trail again!

R.L.S. again?
Yes, he's back. After a brief but intense case of Polynesian paralysis, we're on the trail of *The Treasure* again and R.L.S. is at the helm.
The blessed Bull prodded us into action--again. I rowed out to Hispaniola in record time. Beth was lazing about mostly naked on the cabin roof when the dinghy bumped into the side of the sailboat.
"Hey, who dat banging on my hull?" She propped herself up on one elbow and smiled in my direction.
"Brer Rabbit. Hit the deck and hoist the

sails Foxy Sister. It's anchors aweigh time. Brer Bull is on the island and hot on our trail." I threw my back pack over the rail and tethered the dinghy to a cleat.

"You're kidding," she said indignantly as she sat up and wrapped a towel around herself. "How could he find us here? Did the Gendarme snitch?"

"No, I think the Gendarme is cool." I swung on board. "As far as figuring out where to look for us, I guess this is the first stop this side of the West coast--aside from Hawaii--and we wouldn't go there after eluding the Coast Guard. So I suppose it was only logical."

As I talked I pitched my back pack below and started clearing the decks to sail. Beth slipped on a pair of shorts and a tank top before attacking the sail covers. "Well I think it's pretty rude--I was thinking it was about time we took advantage of those palm trees." she declared.

"Aye, rude indeed--I guess it'll have to be Tuamotan palm trees." Then a thought occurred to me. "Wait just a minute." I stood up and surveyed the shore-line of the bay. "Not a little boat in sight. We can take our time."

"What?" Beth asked with a puzzled expression.

"There aren't any boats around for Bully to come out in. We can take our time and square things away properly before setting sail."

"Can't he just swim out like we've done?"

"Unless he's taken some Red Cross classes; Bully can't swim."

"I can't see him taking swimming lessons, but how do you know?"

"I had to rescue him once when he fell out of a boat back home. I guess he would of died if someone didn't pull him out."

Beth had finished removing the main-sail cover, she brought it back and tossed it down the companionway onto the berth. "So this is interesting, how did it happen?" she asked, leaning against the main boom.

I was leading the starboard sheet back to the cockpit. "Oh, I was home on leave, after Vietnam. Bully had been in and out of the Marines by then. Anyway, he was out in the bay crabbing by himself, and I happened to be watching him pull a pot when he slipped or tripped or something, and fell over the side. The way he was splashing around, it was obvious that he wasn't going to make it. So I dragged him out."

Beth shook her head, "Poor Bully, that must have been really humiliating. So is this why he's being such a pest now?"

"Could be part of it I guess. Sometimes people hate their rescuer. There he is now--you can ask him."

Bully had appeared on the cliff that flanked the west side of the bay. There was an old stairway and landing cut into it. "Yee Ha!" he yelled jubilantly as he stomped down the steps. "Ahoy Jack Assssterd and his little Lady Bethsheeeeba!" He shouted across the hundred yards of graciously intervening water. "We meet again!"

Beth stopped and glared in his direction as I started taking the cover off the mizzen. "Why don't you leave us alone?" Beth shouted back.

"Leave ya alone? If'n thet's what ya wants, why thet's what yer gonna be gettin'. But do the law 'round here know thet ya are on the lam? An do they know why you fine folks are down here in the fust place?" He paused to let his threat soak in, or catch his breath, and then continued. "I didn't think so. Now paddle your sweet little ass over here and pick me up so's we can have ourselves a little pow-wow. From now on things are goin' ta be a whole lot easier."

"All right, all right," I said. "But you'll have to go around to the other side," I pointed to the jetty on the other side of the bay. "There's too much wave action where you are."

"It's OK," Bully eyed the water dubiously. "I can just jump into the boat if you get close."

"That's what I'm afraid of. You'd sink the dinghy if you did that--and these are shark waters!" I added for the fun of it.

He studied the waves frothing around his landing. "Awright. Just over there?" He pointed across the bay.

I nodded. "Yup."

"Awright. But it too damned hot for all this hikin' aroun'." He slapped his face. "Bugs too." He turned and trudged up the steps, shouldered his giant back-pack at the top and trudged off.

I jumped down the cockpit steps and fitted the crank into the diesel.

"What are you doing?" Beth squinted down the companionway. "You're not really going to pick him up are you?"

I looked up. "First answer; starting the engine. Second answer; did Hell freeze over?"

She frowned, "Not that I know of."

"Then no. Not in this life time. I just wanted to stop his bellowing, and a little exercise will do him good."

"Yeah, if he doesn't have a heart attack. I'll start pulling in the anchor line. What about the dinghy?"

"We'll tow it for awhile." I turned the engine over twice and closed the compression releases. She chugged to life. "Good old Lady Di." I patted her valve cover affectionately before closing the access door.

On deck Beth had taken the slack out of the anchor rode. I took over for the vertical lift while she went to take the helm.

As I broke the anchor out, Bully appeared on the far end of the concrete jetty. "Anchor's aweigh," I called back to Beth as I sloshed the mud off before bringing it on deck.

Beth slipped the diesel in gear and started a slow turn to port, towards the jetty. Bully walked faster, almost jogging. I sat down on the forward hatch cover to watch as Beth did a lazy turn to starboard as if she was going to come along side the jetty.

I could see Bully's flaming red face. The sweat was streaming down from his dirty "Cat" ball cap. It was obvious that he thought he'd made his point and was finally gaining his objective. Then Beth advanced the throttle sending a little cloud of diesel smoke his way and Hispaniola towards the harbor entrance. His face fell instantly and as the distance between us widened he stopped and dropped his back-pack.

"You Biiiitch!" he yelled. "Here's for youuu!" He turned around, dropped his pants and bent over, glaring at us from between his legs.

"Oh isn't that cute, he's mooning us." Beth commented as I joined her in the cockpit. She waved sweetly, "Have you ever seen such a hairy ass?"

"No, can't say as I have."

"What will the neighbors think?"

"They'll understand. Mooning is an old Polynesian custom. I wonder if Bully knows that."

"We could make another pass and so you could ask him."

"No, he might just have a hand grenade in

Pacific Gold

that back-pack."

"OK," she continued seaward. "You going to hoist some sail or were you thinking of motoring to the Tuamotus?'

"Good idea. Sails that is."

So, we were off again. Next stop: the *Dangerous Archipelago*, the Tuamotus, and the Sea Gull Island group. It is fairly easy to locate the Tuamotus. They are shown on any reasonable map of the South Pacific. After finding them I can even spot them on an old Dime Store globe. Look just south the equator in the mid eastern part of the big blue Pacific Ocean and there they are. A whole bunch of little dots that could be mistaken for fly specks-- but to the knowledgeable those little dots are the *Dangerous Archipelago!* And a few of those dots represent the Sea Gull Group--and one of *those* dots is our *Treasure Island!*

But which one? That was the question which plagued me. I could sail around the Tuamotus with my shovel for years and not stick it into the right island. But how many old emergency landing strips could there be? Two? Three? Five? Ten? I was mentally prepared to dig up several. But, how do you find a fifty year old, abandoned, emergency landing strip? Or was it abandoned? It could have grown and become a real airport--or it could have just grown bushes and palm trees. Which would be worse? Kind of hard to visualize being able to quietly dig up one end of a runway between flights--even if they were only once a week. On the other hand, an overgrown abandoned landing strip might be hard to recognize on islands that are mostly long and flat.

So we were finally on the home stretch, heading for the *Dangerous Archipelago!* And I was getting worried. I stared at the chart waiting for a clue, an inspiration, a sign--ESP?--anything to tell me which way to go.

"So, what'cha doin' *Capitaine?*" Beth was peering down the companionway from the cockpit.

"Ah....navigating."

"Sooo, what heading should I steer?"

".....Southwest."

"Hmmm, Southwest. Exactly Southwest...or just sort of generally Southwest?"

I looked up at her.

"Jacky, you've been staring at that chart for an hour. What's up?"

"Well.....the time has come when we really need to know just exactly which of the seventy-eight Tuamotu Islands is *our* Treasure Island. But right now I'd settle for the Sea Gull Group--assuming of course that it's not just another name for the whole damn archipelago."

"Hmmmm....I see, yes....sort of a technical difficulty."

"So...."

"So, we just shoot for the middle and see what we find?"

"I guess that's one idea."

"But not a very good one?"

"As good as any, but....how about if we head for a populated island and ask around?"

"You, ask for directions? Whoa, Jacky-boy this is capital "S", serious. What's a good populated one, and better yet--how do we get there?"

I flipped through the *Sailing Directions*, "Here, *Rangiroa*. "...the largest and most populated island in the archipelago..." How does that sound?"

"Great! Now, if only I had a course to steer..."

Pacific Gold

"...it lies about twenty miles westward of *Arutua*." I continued reading.

"OK. Is that statute or nautical miles?"

"Ahhh nautical--of course it's nautical--we're nautical aren't we? So it must be." I slammed shut the *Sailing Directions for The Pacific Islands, volume III*, for emphasis.

"Now, Miss Oyl, if you'll just keep this craft pointed in the general direction of *Arutua*, this Sailorman will consult the chart for a course."

"Miss Oyl? What does that make you? Popeye? Or Bluto?"

"I yam what I yam."

I laid one end of the parallel ruler on *Hiva Oa* and pointed the other at *Rangiroa*, then walked it over to the nearest compass rose. (It slipped, so I had to do it over.) And then squinted to read the tiny numerals, subtracted eleven degrees of magnetic variation, added four degrees for compass error, rounded off to the nearest five degrees, and triumphantly announced, "Two hundred and forty degrees!"

"Aye, aye Captain. Two-four-oh it is. On to the *Dangerous Archipelago!*"

CHAPTER 12: Rangiroa

• *0400 2 December Crs: 45 degrees*
Spd: 2 knts Dpth: O.S. Wx: trades
Helmsman: R.L.S.
Comments: Just changed watch--moonlight, almost cold (I must be getting acclimated.)

We sailed on. The skies were blue. Fluffy trade-wind clouds chased each other from East to West. Friendly following seas pushed us onward. With all sail flying and the wind vane set, there wasn't much to do except watch Hispaniola sail. So: we navigated, took bucket baths on deck, ate, slept, made love, and waited for the atolls of the Dangerous Archipelago to appear over the Western horizon.

That is, until the day Beth awoke from her afternoon nap, and swung her feet into a few inches of water on the floor. "Kersplash." (I was reclining up on the foredeck in the shade of the genny at the time.)

"EEEYOW! Jack! Jack we're sinking!" Beth's cry shattered the peace and tranquility.

I stumbled to my feet, banged a shin on the cabin roof, and hurried aft. Beth was in cockpit staring down at the water sloshing about in our living/dining/bed room.

"I can't tell how fast it's coming in. I just woke up and, and there it was."

"Hmmm." Yes, there it was alright, swirling and sloshing about over the floor boards. I tried to think if I'd forgotten to pump the bilge for several days, but no, it was part of the routine. Brush the teeth, wash the face, pump the bilge, etc...

"Jack, it's getting deeper."

"Right." I climbed down into the swirling bilge water, grabbed the pump handle, settled down on the floor, and commenced pumping.(The pump is handily located on the floor so it was under water. I suppose it was more efficient that way. It certainly made for less pleasant pumping, so I was more efficient.) I always count the strokes when I pump. It's kind of a Zen thing--like counting breaths while meditating. And, in theory anyway, it would indicate how much water was in the boat; but I always lose count.

"Jack, where are the life vests?"

I lost count. "Life vests? Up forward, somewhere in the forepeak. But we're not really sinking. The water level is going down so we are unsinking. It must be a smallish leak. I'm sure we can get it under control."

Squish--squish, squish--squish, the pump put the water back in the ocean while I thought about what to do next. We hadn't hit anything or been attacked by any mad whale fish, so a hole in the side wasn't likely. Some caulking may have come loose from between the planks... The stuffing box where the prop shaft went through the hull might have loosened up... One or more of the through hulls could be leaking...

Fifteen long minutes later the pump sucked air. I turned to see a worried looking Beth, wearing an orange life jacket, peering down from the cockpit. "Do you want me to pump while you check things out?"

It didn't appear that we were sinking very rapidly. "Only if it comes over the floor boards again."

I worked systematically from the bow towards the stern, opening cupboards, looking behind drawers, checking the hull and through hull valves and everything I could see for incoming wetness. Finally I reached the engine compartment in the stern. the prop shaft appeared to be in good order. But there *was* a trickle of water. There behind the engine, in the deepest, darkest, most awkward, cramped place in the whole boat is a through-hull for an aft bilge pump that I had never used. I turned the flashlight towards it. The hose had come off the through-hull and the ball valve handle was in the open position. As I watched, a following sea caught up with us a cup, or so, of sea water splashed in.

"Ah ha!"

"Ah ha?" A hopeful echo came from topsides.

"Ah ha, I've spotted the culprit." I declared as I extricated myself from the belly of the whale (or perhaps the bowels.) Sweating through a coating of greasy engine soot, oil, and rust, and more than slightly queasy, I wobbled up the steps into the cockpit.

"So, what and/or where is this culprit?"

I took several deep breaths of fresh ocean air

while gazing at the horizon, then pointed and said, "Through-hull. Down there."

Beth considered that bit of information respectfully and then asked hopefully, "Can we fix it?"

"Sure." I took another deep breath and looked at the horizon some more. "I'll have to go down in there." I pointed to the little hatch cover under the tiller. "We'll disengage the wind vane. Then, if you can lift the tiller and steer, I'll open hatch, stand on my head in there, and close the valve. We never use that bilge pump anyway."

"Just sort of a safety thing huh."

"Yeah, one of those things you don't really need but if you ignore it long enough it'll try to kill you."

"Right. Or in this case sink us." Beth looked significantly at the saloon floor. "Shall we get to it."

I followed her gaze to where the water was creeping above the floor boards. "Right."

Beth took the tiller. I disengaged the wind vane. Then she stood off to the side on the cockpit seat and raised the tiller as high as she could and still steer. I opened the little hatch and wedged my arms, head, and shoulders into the two foot by two foot opening. I could touch the lever on the sea cock, but couldn't move it. Scrunching deeper into the little hatchway, "OK...you slimy s.o.b.," I muttered into the bilge as the tips my fingers reached under the lever and pulled up. Reluctantly it moved to the closed position.

I eased back out, trying to leave as little of my skin as possible on the various protruding bolt heads and etc... Slamming the little hatch cover and rubbing my forearm, I pronounced the job, "Done."

"That's it?" Beth asked as she lowered the tiller.

"Yup, except for pumping the rest of the water back into the ocean." I said, hoping I was right. "You can put the wind vane back to work now if you want."

"I think I'll steer for awhile." She unzipped her life jacket. "But maybe I won't need this." She grinned sheepishly. "That was quite a shock to wake up to."

"Yeah." I agreed as I went below to pump again. "I'm sure glad it is daytime."

"Oh God, yes."

We checked the bilge more often and peered suspiciously at any dampness about the floor boards for awhile, but the problem was cured. *Hispaniola* kept rolling along as an endless supply of swells came up astern, each giving us a little push towards *Treasure Island*. The sun was hot in the daytime; the stars brilliant at night. It was a cosmic forever thing, a continuum lasting until the end of forever. It felt like we would be a part of it in some manner until then. We sailed our little boat and observed the sunsets. Life was simple. Life was good. The moon had been about half full when we made our unscheduled departure. Now, with each sunset, it was further West and growing. By the time we were in the proximity of the *Dangerous Archipelago* it would ripen to give us a good landfall moon. I mentioned this to Beth while we lingered over a tot of sunset rum.

"Of course." she replied. "We're in sync with the universe. When the moon is full we'll make landfall and I'll have my period."

I looked at her over the rim of my cracked coffee cup and wisely agreed, "Of course. If you're in sync with the universe the rest is obvious." I leaned back against the cabin and gazed at the moon ascending over the rudder post. "So, I'd say it should be full tomorrow night."

"Me too. We'll be looking at the Tuamotus tomorrow night Matey." She took a slug of her rum for emphasis.

I drank down my rum before stating, "Aye, and it will be with mixed feelings for sure."

"Aye." she agreed. And then, after a moment asked, "Why?"

I uncapped the bottle that had been rolling about on the cockpit grating and poured each of us another inch of dark rum. "Well, it's back to reality again isn't it? This is the way life should be. But it isn't. On shore the simplicity vanishes and this is just a beautiful dream."

"Maybe this is the reality and that's the dream." She countered.

"Of course. That's true. When we're here, this is reality; when we're there, this is dream. The day after tomorrow we'll step ashore into a new reality and this will have been a nice dream."

She studied the rum in her cup, "I wonder what that reality will be?"

"Ah yes, that's the question isn't. Will we find a clue to the location of the Sea Gull Group of Islands and ultimately Treasure Island? Will the natives be friendly or ass holes. Will Bully be there to threaten us with incarceration and castration by the EPA?"

"Bully?" Beth nearly spilled her rum. "You don't think that he'll be there do you?

"Pourquoi pas? San Francisco? Atu Ona? Why not Rangiroa?"

"Then why are we going there?"

I considered a moment or two, "Well, to find out where to go next."

"But, isn't there another island that would

work just as well?"

"I suppose so. I guess I feel it doesn't matter."

"Hmmm, you mean like wherever we go Bully will too, or if Bully's going to pick a destination for us we'll show up there?"

"Something like that, yeah. So, I propose that we make this stay as short as possible. He always seems to be a couple of days behind us. Maybe this time we can get out of town before he gets in."

"Good idea. I think he may be getting tired of standing on shore and watching as we sail away."

I drained my cup again and considered. "Yes, there is a possibility that he may be more devious in the future."

Beth drained her cup. "Devious and nasty." She set her cup down decisively. "This will be strictly a business stop. It doesn't matter how nice it is, we won't linger. No fooling around under the palm trees. There'll be plenty of time for that *after* we get the treasure in our hold. Right Cap'n?"

"Right-o Matey!" I thumped my cup down alongside hers.

Being a prudent mariner, I took sights on Venus, Acrux and the Moon at sunrise just to confirm that our calculations were right. That evening there was a thin line of palm trees silhouetted in the setting sun.

"By the Great Horned Spoon, I believe we have a Land Ho!" Beth proclaimed. We were having our sundown tot of rum on the foredeck reclining against the cabin on either side of the mast--she to starboard and me to port.

"Mmmmm yes, or one might say Palm Ho! But what's a Great Horned Spoon?"

Pacific Gold

"I'm not sure, but that's what Erck the Viking always used to say. But I'm afraid he never had the occasion to say 'Palm Ho'."

The sun had finished dropping into the ocean; Beth twisted around and gazed aft. "There's the full moon, right on schedule."

"When everything is right, can anything be wrong?" I asked rhetorically.

"No." she answered definitely.

"Then I shouldn't worry as whether those palm trees are rooted in the sand of the correct island? Or how far away they might be? And whether we'll arrive in the dark or daylight?"

She considered for a moment, then replied, "We know it's the right island. It's the one that we've been steering for all week. And....we'll arrive with the sun. Got anymore rum?"

I poured another inch into our cups. "I like your certainty, but I think I'll worry a little anyway."

"I'll feel better if you do." She held out her cup. "A toast. To our first Palm Fall!"

"Aye!" I clinked her cup again and drained mine. "And many happy returns of the same."

"Aye aye."

Actually, things did work out about the way Beth predicted, or they would have if I wouldn't have reduced sail a couple of hours before dawn. That put us a couple of hours away from the island at dawn and three hours from the pass through the reef. But that was OK as we had to wait another hour off the entrance to *Passe Tiputa* for the tidal current to slacken. We might have waited just a little longer, but with the motor roaring and the sails full we slowly powered against the flow into the lagoon.

Once inside, we sailed easily over to the village of *Tiputa*. After rowing ashore, we chatted with the *Gendarme* (who showed no undo interest in our presence,) purchased some fresh French bread (Yummy!) and ate a couple of big hunks walking back to Hispaniola.

Tiputa didn't look promising for our quest so we decided to cross to the other side of the pass where we could see several (seven) sail boats anchored in front of a resort. (The baker had told us it was the *Kia Ora Hotel*.)

A couple of people waved from anchored boats as we passed by. One of them was a naked man doing something on the foredeck of a boat of French registry. We anchored comfortably close to shore and the other vessels.

"Attire is casual here." Beth commented.

Which was true. When we went ashore we found that many of the French tourist ladies left their bikini tops in there suit cases. "They last longer that way." I explained to Beth as I admired the custom.

"Which, the tops or the looks?"

"Ah, yes." I replied, tardily forcing my eyes back to her.

"Well, if you think I'm going to join in the local custom, you're wrong."

"When in Rome...." I suggested meekly.

"Forget it. I'm not one of these Free French. Besides, we have a mission--remember? In and out quickly."

"Right."

"And I don't think any of these topless honeys will have the answer we need."

"Hmmm, no probably not." I agreed regretfully. "What we need are sailors, or fishermen, or English speaking Tuamotans."

"So where do we find those?"

"Well, you could interview that guy on the boat who waved?" I suggested.

"No."

Pacific Gold

"I know where we'll be able to find sailors a little later." We had been walking along the white sand beach and were now coming to the hotel proper. It was made up of thatched huts by the lagoon. Set back a little distance was a restaurant. There was another little building located by a swimming pool. I pointed, "There, at the bar."

"Ah ha, right you are. In the mean time, why don't we sample the fare in the dining room?"

"Pourquoi pas? Why not indeed?"

Beth locked my arm firmly in hers. "Besides, the waiter may know something." I gave her a questioning look. "They do in *my* books."

The waiter just specialized in good food and wine. A couple of hours later we took possession of a couple of bar stools in the little thatch drinking establishment. I asked for a mai tai but it wasn't on the menu. Neither was the pinã collada that Beth desired. We ended up with *une bière et vin blanc.*

"What the heck, we're here on business anyway."

"Santé." I raised my beer.

Beth countered with, *"Skoal!"*

We sipped our drinks. It might be a long evening and we didn't want to get plastered; just in case we found out something. There were already a few people there with others slowly trickling in. Most nodded to us and some asked about our voyage or politely complimented Hispaniola. By dark there were fifteen or twenty people present. Someone was playing an acoustic guitar and a person across the room was singing.

Beth was talking with a woman on her left. "It looks like most of the tourists are elsewhere."

The woman laughed, "Only hotel employees and yachties come down here." She spoke with what I guessed to be a Scandinavian accent. "You just sailed in today?"

"Yes. We were a week from Marquesas Islands. Are you on a boat?"

"No. But I sail. I, ah, jump ship here. It's really a nice place....and the boat....it was not so nice."

"The Captain didn't mind?"

"He minded....but....he is not so nice either. It did not matter whether he minded or not. I quit."

"Ah." Beth nodded knowingly.

"Where are Marquesas Islands?"

As Beth explained I ordered another beer and wondered how she arrived in the Tuamotu Islands without passing by the Marquesas Islands. But, I guessed she wasn't navigating. Obviously this lady wasn't going to tell us what we needed to know. The large, dark skinned bartender appeared to be a local. When he brought my new Heineken I asked. "Have you lived in the Tuamotus long?"

"*Oui*. I am Paumotan by birth. I was born Takaroa. What part United States do you live in?"

"Oregon. It's on the Pacific coast."

"Ah. It is cold there, no?"

"Well no, but colder than here."

His white teeth flashed when he smiled knowingly. "I met a man a few days ago from Oregon. He said it was *tres* cold there. *Beaucoup la neige*...ahhhh....snow! I have not seen snow, but it must be very cold to have frozen water laying about on the ground. No?"

My heart skipped a beat. "This man, do you know his name."

"*Non, non.*" he declared shaking his head.

"Boat people, they come and go....too fast."

"He was on a boat then. Was he a big man with a red face?"

"*Oui,* on a boat I think. Big? *Non,* I think not." He made an indefinite hand gesture. "Not big." And went off to wait on another customer.

Beth jabbed me in the ribs. "Do you think it was Bully?" she whispered.

"Hard to tell. I hope not. It didn't sound like him. And I don't think he'd be on a boat."

"But he was from Oregon. Let's find out what we need to know and scram."

"Right." I surveyed the clientele. A group in the corner was intent on making some kind of music. The guitar had been passed to another, others were thumping on the table or tapping glasses and singing. Everyone seemed to be having a good time except a small, dark looking fellow sitting alone at a table in the corner. I had the feeling that he was watching us, but it may have been that he was just watching everyone. No one appeared to pay any attention to him.

I leaned across Beth and asked her neighbor, "Do you know who the dark little man in the corner is?"

She shivered and without looking said, "He is the Captain of the boat I was on. Pay no attention to him."

"He's still keeping an eye on you?"

"Pay no attention to him. He is crazy."

Beth signaled the waiter for another glass of wine. When he brought it she asked, "Do you know where the Sea Gull Islands are?"

He looked at her with a puzzled expression as he picked up my francs for the drink. "Where the Sea Girl Islands are?" He repeated hopefully. Obviously wondering if she was making a joke.

"No, the Sea Gull Islands. You know, like the

bird--Sea Gull." She said very distinctly coinciding with one of those random quiet moments that happens in every group of people.

"Ah," said the woman next to Beth knowingly. "The Sea Gull Islands."

"Mais non Madame. I have not heard of these islands." He turned to the room at large. "Has anyone know of Sea Bird Islands?"

Oh shit, I thought. So much for doing this quietly. "The Sea *Gull* Islands." I corrected hopefully.

The pause extended as several people shook their heads and one asked, "Is that off the Irish coast, in the North Sea?"

"Ah, no. I hope not." This brought general laughter and the return of conversation.

I shrugged my shoulders and turned back to the bartender. He shrugged and went off to fill another order. We finished our drinks and quietly got up to leave. An older man sitting near the door stopped me with a hand on my arm.

"I may have heard or read about them. Why do you want to know?"

I was ready for the question just in case it was ever asked. Nothing like the truth. "My Uncle was there during the war. He said they were really nice. I thought I'd stop by since I was in the neighborhood. If I can figure out which ones they are. They are not on my charts."

"You're off that ketch that came in today aren't you?"

I nodded. "Yes."

"Give me a little time. I'll let you know if I figure out where I heard of them. That was the Sea Gull Islands?"

"Right." I shook his hand. "And thank you."

He waved me off as I followed Beth out the door.

Pacific Gold

The next afternoon as I was resting up after putting the hose back on the aft bilge-pump, (Beth had thought it wise to go ashore while I cursed into the bilge.) the old man paddled over in his inflatable.

"Ahoy *Hispaniola*!"

"Ahoy yourself." I said taking his painter. "Come aboard. I was just having a warm beer, would you like one?"

"Ah, the coin of the realm. Yes indeed." He replied as he clambered spryly aboard. "Barney, Barney Applebye." He introduced himself as he extended his hand.

"John Astor." I replied shaking his hand.

"John Astor. I say that's a famous name you have there. Like your boat's. Hispaniola."

"Yes," I handed him the bottle of warm beer. "Famous names, but not famous individuals."

"*Hispaniola*'s from Stevenson's book, *Treasure Island*, isn't it? I saw it when you came in and remarked it to Martha. That's the Mrs."

"Yes, I thought that it was a good name for a boat." I replied, wishing that I had named her anything else at the moment.

Barney took a drink and wiped the sweat from his forehead with a dingy white handkerchief. "That's kind of what a boat is, isn't it? We invest our treasure in it anyway." He chuckled at his joke and I smiled to indicate that I got it. "You'll have to forgive me, I'm a retired professor of literature and intellectual stimulation of the literary kind is rare here."

"Yes, I guess that it is. But say, maybe you'll know. Is there a library here?"

"Here? You mean on this island? Rangiroa?" He paused, struck by the question. "What an extraordinary question. Another good question. I don't know the answer. I never thought of it, but they might, mightn't they. This is the most populated island in the Archipelago. We'll have to check it out. Ha, check it out! I doubt they would let a yachty do that! These French are so possessive. But it would be worth a look, yes indeed."

He took another small drink and gave forth a petit belch. "One thing about warm beer-- have to drink it slow. Otherwise it goes straight to the head." He tapped his bald pate. "Unless, of course, that is the desired effect!"

He laughed again and I wondered how long he planned on staying--the afternoon was young. "A library, you must be very fluent in French to want to visit a library here. A rare thing in an American yachty." He saluted me with his bottle.

"No, not really. I just thought I might find out about my islands there."

"Ah...Ah yes." He responded with a tinge of disappointment in his voice. "Good idea though." He immediately brightened. "Which, brings us to the express purpose of my visit. You won't need to go to *le bibliothèque* for that." He shook his head. "Indeed no, as enticing a prospect as that might be. No, I have located your Sea Gull Islands."

I stared in amazement. "Really? Where?"

"Do you have Publication 80, entitled; *Sailing Directions for The Pacific Islands*, volume III?"

"The Sailing Directions? Yes, yes I have them." I dashed below for the book, knowing that there was no mention of the Sea Gull Islands in it.

"Here it is," I said, offering the book to the Professor.

He waved it away. "I don't have my glasses.

Pacific Gold

I never take them in the dinghy. Shouldn't want to lose them you know. Turn to page one hundred and three."

I did as he said.

"Now look for paragraph four dash sixty eight."

I did, and there they were! I read, "Raevski, (Sea Gull) Islands." I stared in disbelief. "How did I ever miss that?"

Barney shrugged, "Probably from poor study habits learned in elementary school."

Now I stared at him. I couldn't believe he was lecturing me on my poor study habits. But, then again, he was probably right, and what did I care anyway? Here were my Islands! And according to the book there were only three of them! I closed the book and reached down for another bottle. "Another beer Barney?" I said handing it to him. "Thank you, thank you very much."

He finished his beer and accepted the replacement while I struggled to contain my excitement. Actually I, ungratefully, wanted to throw him off the boat, raise anchor, and get underway. I looked toward the beach. Where was Beth?

Instead I had another beer and directed the conversation in other directions--which wasn't hard with Barney.

We quietly slipped out of the anchorage under the cover of darkness. Not really for stealth, though it felt like it, rather because that was when the tide was right to sail out the pass with some measure of control. Not that I minded. I was none too comfortable about how public our destination had become. The nearly full moon lighted our way as we sailed serenely out through the pass.

Chapter 13: At Sea--Again

• *0600, 2 December   Pos: S14°44', W147°38'
(About 15 miles due north of Tiputa Pass)
Crs: 045°   Spd: 2knts(maybe)   Dpth: O.S.
Helmsman: J. J. Astor
Comments: adrift*

I've taken charge of this helm! Big deal, we're no closer to Treasure Island today than yesterday (actually a bit farther away.) I took morning sights to confirm our position, these islands *are* the *Dangerous Archipelago* so the prudent mariner.... Good thing! It seems that we are five miles west of where I thought, and getting farther all the time. I forgot to allow for the 10 to 20 knot (per day) current from the East, shown on the pilot chart.

There's not much I can do about it at the moment. With a very light Easterly trade-wind the best course we can steer is about forty-five

Pacific Gold

degrees magnetic with a resulting track of true North. If we went onto the port tack, and conditions stayed the same, we could expect to anchor back at the hotel in time for supper. "Hmmm... No. Bad idea."

* *1200, 2 December   Pos:S14°38', W147°41' (or a little north and west of where we were 6 hours ago.) Crs: ? (Would like to go 045°.)*
Spd: nil--2 knts Dpth: O.S.
Helmsman: Pacific Ocean
Comments: What the....?

Things didn't stay the same, they got worse. By ten o'clock the wind died altogether.

"I guess that we are not exactly racing towards the finish line, are we?" Beth observed as we finished breakfast.

"Not exactly..." I agreed.

"Nobody said treasure hunting would be easy."

"Or fast."

"Or fast."

"This sort of thing requires patience."

"Maybe we should crank up the old motor and just steam on over there?"

"Too far. And I want to save the fuel for maneuvering in the lagoon if we have to."

"Hmmm, I suppose that would be worse. To get to the right island and not be able to get in would be *Dantésque* to say the least."

"Done with that?" I was in the cockpit rinsing the bowls in a bucket of sea water.

She handed me her bowl and spoon. "Gee, I didn't realize it could be this calm out on the ocean." Beth was staring off towards the horizon in the general direction of Rangiroa. "This is like being in the lagoon. Too bad we're not--we could go swimming."

"Yeah, it is like a big swimming pool......why can't we go swimming?" I handed the last bowl to her to dry and put away. "We're just drifting. Yeah! Let's have a swim!"

I lowered the limp genoa onto the foredeck, sheeted the main and mizzen in tight, tossed the ends of the sheets over the rails--to grab just in case the boat started to sail away without us--stripped off my shorts and dove over the side just as Beth was coming out of the cabin.

Already airborne, I heard her call out, "Hey!"

Hey? I thought as plunged deeply into the marvelous blue water.

"Hey what?" I asked when I surfaced.

"Hey, I see we don't need swimming suits," she commented. Then added, "Hey, isn't it awfully deep?"

I thought a moment. "About a mile."

"Statute or nautical?" she asked, stalling.

"Nautical, definitely nautical. Come on in, it's great." I turned over and floated on my back with my ears below the water line. It was so nice, the water fresh and cool; the sky blazing blue-white; the sun hot on my face and other body parts above the water line. I heard her voice so I raised my head and went back to treading water. "What?"

"Have you seen any fish?"

Ah, interpret that to mean *sharks*. "No, but that's a good idea. Could you please get me my mask and flippers?"

She disappeared and reappeared a couple of moments later with them. After putting them on I scanned the under-water world for fish (and anything else.) There were a couple of little ones (pilot fish?) hanging around the prop and rudder. Other than that it was just limitless blue water, deepening in color as it deepened in

Pacific Gold

depth. My shadow went down into infinity surrounded by rays of sunlight; like a 3D star burst with me in the middle. "Wow." I commented into my snorkel.

"What?" I heard Beth say from the boat. "Wow what?"

I raised my head up to look at Beth through my mask which immediately began fogging up. "I said, Wow."

"Wow what?"

I spit out the snorkel. "Wow, it's incredibly beautiful! Come on in!"

"Are there any fish?"

"Just a couple of little ones back by the rudder. You won't bother them." (It was nearly impossible to not to say the "S" word, but I managed.)

"You're sure."

"Yup. Nobody else around." (Especially *Jaws!*)

She nervously glanced around the horizon before pulling off her tee shirt and plunging feet first into the pool.

"Ooooo," she squealed when she surfaced. "I've never been skinny dipping before."

I laughed, "I think you have to be a teenager for it to be skinny dipping. I think when you're our age it's just swimming naked."

She swam off about ten yards. "So, I'm a teenager." Then turned over to kick back like a motor boat. "It's dee-licious! That's what it is."

She was right. Swimming naked (or skinny dipping) in the middle of a warm, calm ocean is delicious. We swam, floated, inspected the hull (it was growing a little weed here and there, nothing serious.)

Then a few warning puffs from an approaching breeze prompted us to scamper back on board. I raised the genny and slacked the main and mizzen sheets. Slowly, very slowly; magically the sails filled and Hispaniola resumed our voyage. It wasn't exactly in, or even close to the right direction but we were sailing just the same.

• *1800, December 2 Pos: S14°25', W147°29'*
Crs: 135° Spd: 5 knts! Dpth: O.S.
Helmsman: J. J. Astor & P. Ocean
Comments: Sailing again!

We nearly ran off the chart to the North so we tacked. All things being equal, we can stay on this course for sixty miles or until six a.m., whichever comes first. Squalls on the horizon. Guess we'll be keeping watch tonight.

Beth thought she saw a boat when we were drying off in the sun. But she only saw whatever it was once, and just for a moment. When she tried to point it out to me, it was gone. It was probably a fishing boat from Rangiroa. If it was a boat, it was the first we've seen at sea since we left the shipping lanes behind. Lots of room in this Great Southern Ocean.

• *0200, December 3   Pos: S14°58', W147°13'*
Crs:045° Spd: 4 to 6 knts Dpth: O.S.
Helmsman: JJA, PO, & Squalls
Comments: squalling

Well, we didn't go sixty miles and it's not six a.m., but we just tacked. We came about involuntarily in a squall, so we'll go this way for awhile.

The first little squall arrived just before sundown. They have been getting progressively worse. The last one was full fledged, complete

Pacific Gold

with thunder and lightning. Fortunately we were only carrying the jib and mizzen sail, having furled the main early on. The first squall was sort of pleasant and we rinsed the salt off in the rain. The last was vicious with big cold rain drops and strong shifting winds.

The result after four have passed over us, is that I don't know where we are. And we are in treacherous waters. So this new tack into open water is a good idea. We can always tack back after daylight.

Time to wake-up Beth. I'm sure she'll be happier sailing into open water too. She went to lay down about ten saying that she wouldn't be able to sleep, but she hasn't reappeared. I hope she's been asleep, it would be nice if one of us is not tired.

- *1900, December 3   Pos: S14°35', W146°17'*
Crs: 060°   Spd: 4 knts   Dpth: O.S.
Helmsman: B & J
Comments: Ignorance is sleep

Beth had been asleep. She missed the whole lightening show. That was good as she would have been worried. (Not that I wasn't! The idea of sailing a lightning rod through a thunderstorm is unnerving. Ben Franklin I'm not.)

"Do you want me to sit up with you for awhile?" I asked as Beth made herself comfortable in cockpit. She had her flashlight, sweater, rain coat, and a cup of hot tea.

"No why?" She asked as she squinted at the dimly lit compass. "Hey, we're on a new course."

"Yeah, after the last squall the wind stayed southeast. So we can finally steer a little better course."

"Sixty degrees?"
"Right. So you slept after all?"
"Like a log. I must have been really tired."
"Ah, the virtues of clean living."
She cocked her head to one side and looked at me. "Jacky, I think it's time you got some sleep."
"OK." I went below and was about to crawl between the sheets.
"How come we don't have the main up?" Beth asked.
"Well, it's been kind of squally."
"Oh......would you mind if I raised it. The weather looks good now. I can see stars all around."
I finished climbing into bed. "Go ahead if you want to, but keep an eye out for approaching squalls. And be sure to snap on your life line."
"OK Cap'n. Nighty night."
I heard her feet thumping on the roof as she went forward, but I didn't hear her come back because I was asleep.
Beth sailed the night out. When I awoke at eight bells, sunshine was streaming through the port lights and the wind was still steady from the southeast. Out in the cockpit Beth was ninety per-cent naked (she was wearing her big straw hat,) in the bright morning sunlight and busy doing her nails.
She looked up when I came aft to the companionway. "Personal hygiene really takes a beating on a sailboat. Did you see that woman's nails that I was talking to in the bar? She may have arrived on a boat, but it was a long time ago. Her nails were an inch long."
"Really? Guess I didn't notice."
"Well maybe not an inch, but close to it. At least a half an inch."

Pacific Gold

Still sleepy, I couldn't imagine why this was significant. "Want some coffee?" I asked turning toward the stove.

"Of course. But come on outside and clear your head. I'll make breakfast. I've been thinking about having pan-cakes and canned bacon ever since it got light." She said, gathering up her clothing and etc...from about the cockpit.

When I came back from a trip to the foredeck she casually commented, "Oh, it's a good thing we are keeping watches again."

"Because of the squalls?" Good smelling breakfast smoke was wafting out of the galley and my stomach responded with a growl.

"No. I saw boat lights last night."

"Oh, when was that?"

"About an hour after you went to bed. I'd just gotten everything situated and was checking around the horizon before opening my book, and there they were." She stacked four hot-cakes and some bacon on a plate and handed it out to me along with a mug of coffee.

"How close?"

She poured more batter onto the skillet. Hot grease spattered onto her belly, she jumped back. "Ouch." She rubbed her belly with a dish towel. "Oh, not close at all. I just turned on our nav lights and kept an eye out for them. Funny thing; when I first saw them I thought they were coming our way, but after I turned on our lights I couldn't see them anymore."

I picked up a crisp strip of bacon and crunched it between my teeth. Canned bacon is thin, mostly fat, and awfully good at sea. "Mmmmm good idea; hot-cakes and bacon. You should be on the early morning watch more often."

"Don't get any ideas."

"Do you think it was a sailboat? I mean did the lights look like they might be on a mast head, like ours?"

Beth was eating in the galley while cooking more cakes. "Pass the Grandma, please." Our syrup bottle was shaped like a plump, matronly lady wearing an apron. Pure imitation maple syrup. I handed her the sticky bottle.

"No, I don't think so, I think they were too far apart." She paused as she poured the syrup onto her cakes. "No, I don't think they were on a mast, they didn't sway like they would on a mast. But, don't some sailboats have them down on deck too?"

"Yeah, they can be most anywhere. But if they're on a mast then it's pretty certain it is a sailboat. Which sides were they on?"

Beth chewed and thought, turning this way and that, and finally decided. "Red was left, so they would have been coming towards us. Red is on starboard and green is on port--isn't it?"

"Yeah. So whoever it was, was coming towards us, and then disappeared after you turned our lights on. Hmmm..."

We finished our breakfast and spent a leisurely day sailing northeast into the trades. We hadn't done much windward sailing so it was a novel experience to be heeled over and taking the seas on the bow rather than having them push us along on an even keel. I still felt sluggish. We both took naps. Going to weather would take some getting used to.

A fringe of palm trees appeared off the port bow as we were eating supper. "Palm Ho, again." I announced to Beth who was facing sternward.

She twisted around to confirm my sighting. "Which island?"

"Not ours. I think it's *Ahé*, or it might be

Pacific Gold

Manihé. In either case it'll soon be time to tack."

"Good, that'll put the bunk on the down side for the night."

By seven o'clock *Manihe's* palm trees cleared the horizon, dead ahead. *Ahé* was now off our port beam. An excellent time and place to tack.

* 0500, 4 December   Pos: S15°21', W146°03'
Crs: 060°   Spd: 5 knts   Dpth: O.S.
Helmsman: CWO John J. Astor
Comments: Killed anyone lately?

The trade wind remained steady as twilight deepened into night with no signs of impending squalls. Stars and planets loaded the sky with bright pin-pricks of light.

We were reclining in the cockpit with our usual evening tot of rum when Beth asked, "Have you ever killed anyone?"

I choked on my rum, coughed, looked over at Beth, considered, swirled the rum in my coffee cup, shrugged my shoulders, and admitted that I had.

"Thought so--tell me about it."

"I was in the war, remember?"

"Oh, in the war. Of course--well did you kill anyone specifically or just in a general sense?"

"Both, I guess."

"Tell me about it. It's OK, I know that you're not a bad person or anything like that."

I shrugged again and stared into my rum. "OK. Well, in the general sense...that is what we did. Sort of...I mean we took troops out and dropped them off, and they in turn went looking for the enemy. And when they encountered Charley they either captured or killed them, or got killed. And I supported that effort." I took a sip of my rum and considered. Beth waited. "In the specific sense I killed three or four, maybe more."

"As a Warrant Officer I usually didn't have command responsibilities; other than my helicopter and crew. One of the exceptions was guard duty. On guard duty I would be in charge of a half dozen bunkers on the perimeter. It was my job to go around and check on the men to see that they were alive, awake, not too stoned, and etc... We came under attack one night when I was on duty. First they sent in a volley of rockets, then mortar fire... That was fairly common." I took another sip. Remembering back twenty-five years, I could still smell the dust and stink of a perimeter bunker in South Viet Nam. I remembered the fear and adrenalin as we peered through the darkness looking for Charlie to come over the wire as the rockets and mortar shells exploded in the camp behind us.

"What happened then, Jacky?" Beth asked quietly from the darkness across the cockpit.

"Suddenly the sector to our left started blazing away with everything they had. This too was fairly common. Sitting there all night long just waiting, the guys would shoot with the slightest excuse. I still didn't see anything. My radio man was in contact with the other bunkers. They weren't seeing anybody either. By this time one of our helicopters was airborne and dropping flares. He came over our sector, the flare popped illuminating the area in front of us, and there was Charlie coming for us. They started shooting. We opened fire. I shot two, quick and easy--Bam! Bam!"

I took a drink to wash the battle taste out of my mouth. My cup was empty and I searched around the cockpit grating to find the bottle.

"I guess you won, or you wouldn't be here."

Pacific Gold

I found the bottle and poured, using the dim red glow of the compass light to see. "I don't know if *won* is the correct word, but they didn't get through that night. If the flare ship had been a little slower it might have turned out differently." I set my mug down and poured a splash into Beth's.

We drank.

"So what about the others?"

I was tempted to say that was it. That I might have shot a couple more in the fracas. But instead I said, "I may have shot more that night, it was hard to tell. But the other one, for sure, was out at a staging area in the jungle."

"We had about twenty helicopters parked in a meadow waiting to make a troop insertion. We'd been there a couple of hours. It was supposed to be secure; there was an infantry company spread out around us in the jungle. I had the last ship in the formation, (not an enviable slot, but it was mine.)"

"So I was parked at one end of the clearing. In this kind of a waiting situation we often played cards or read or ate c-rations or slept, but I was edgy; on account of my position in the formation I guess. (You see the last ship going into a landing zone was the easiest for the enemy to pick-off.)"

I took a sip of rum thinking about the midday heat of the dry monsoon. The dry elephant grass taller than a man. Especially a man of small physical stature. I could smell the grass again, the helicopter's jet fuel and oil, the dust, the sweat.

"The rest of the crew was doing the usual things, but I took my rifle and sat down in the shadow of the helicopter leaning against the rear cross-tube. I had a book, but didn't open it. Instead I thought about home, and of hunting. (I would sit quietly, like I was, and wait for a deer to show up.) When movement in the tree line caught my eye. My immediate thought was that it was one of our infantry patrols or one of the helicopter guys poking around souvenir hunting (a stupid thing to do, but...waiting like that was pretty boring.) As I watched, whatever it was stealthily climbed a tree. Maybe a tiger, I thought. (I wished I had the scope that was on my hunting rifle back home.) I sighted on the critter anyway--not thinking to shoot. It reached a fork in tree and I realized that I was looking at a man. I still had the idea that he was one of us. Then I saw him raise a rifle and point it in our direction. I already had him sighted in when I saw he wasn't friendly. I squeezed the trigger. Bam! He dropped to the ground like a sack of cement. That's what I thought then, 'Just like a sack of cement.'"

We were quiet for a while. Slowly the stars in the black sky and the water sounds replaced the jungle and the war. "So, was he the enemy?"

"Yeah. NVA sniper. All decked out with a silencer and scope on his Chi-com rifle. He could have had a turkey shoot. I was probably the only person with a clear view of him. And that was just dumb luck or something."

"Hmmm...something...something like The God of the Wind and Sky and Sea Etc...?"

"Perhaps, but why should he favor me? It wasn't my country. I had no business being there."

"You've thought about this."

"Quite a bit."

The silence of the sea noises returned and I leaned my head back against the cabin and looked at Orion. Bold Orion--my friend. The same Orion of long ago above that other part of the world. Beth softly stroked my shoulder.

"So, why do you ask?"

"Well, it seems like something I should know."

"Hmmm."

"I know this sounds dumb, but quite often people get killed or attacked when treasure hunting."

"Ahhh.....No, I'm not going to kill anyone for any treasure."

"I'm sorry Jacky. I didn't mean to stir up old memories that are better forgotten. I guess I didn't think about that."

"It's OK." I gave her a kiss.

She continued stroking my shoulder for awhile, then went below to sleep, leaving me alone with my memories and the stars.

The moon came up about ten, it was lopsided but still big and made lots of light. As I watched it rise, a sail was silhouetted in it.

I rubbed my eyes and it was gone. I dashed below for the binoculars, but the boat, if it had really been there, had disappeared.

Could that have been the same boat that she had seen the night before? Pretty weird to suddenly sight two boats momentarily on consecutive nights after not seeing any for so long. But then if you see one, why not two, or three? Perhaps it was just a case of random clumping? If it was the same one, it didn't have its lights on tonight. It was probably just coincidence, but it didn't feel that way to me.

After a long sleepy day I didn't feel sleepy that night so I drowsed occasionally, but mostly staying alert watching for the next atoll, *Apataki*, to appear.

I sensed it off to the starboard about four AM. An hour later, in the predawn grayness, I could see it.

Quietly, I tacked Hispaniola into open water again. Then, knowing all was well, carefully slipped between the sheets next to Beth and slept.

• *1700, 4 December   Pos: S15°, W145°08'*
Crs: 135° Spd: 5 knts Dpth: O.S.
Helmsman: Hispaniola
Comments: Let the Boat sail!

With a steady wind, Hispaniola sailed herself all day at five knots on an east-northeast course. We slept most of the morning (Beth got up around nine, I about lunch time to take a noon sight.)

I told Beth about the boat I may have seen.

"It's amazing how you can go for weeks without seeing anybody and then suddenly there are boats all over the place," She observed.

"Yes, perhaps even incredible."

By five o'clock we had gone sixty miles and cleared most of the atolls in our way, so we went onto the port tack for the night. Beth likes to sleep with the bed on the down side of the boat; it's easier to cook that way too. (It's good to keep the cook happy.)

• *0000 5 December   Pos: S15°25', W145°02'*
Crs: 060° Spd: 3-4 knts Dpth: O.S.
Helmsman: Davy Jones
Comments: Prudent Mariners keep a sharp lookout.

I just went back onto the starboard tack about five hours earlier than planned. The wind has fallen off and I think we have only gone twenty-five miles since five PM.

Beth made her version of potato pan-cakes

Pacific Gold

for supper. Reconstituted dried potatoes mixed with powdered eggs and powdered milk along with lots of powdered garlic and onion. She diced up a nice succulent can of Spam and threw that into the pan as well. On the other burner she heated up a fresh can of creamed corn "niblets". It didn't taste bad and I'm sure there were plenty of calories to keep us fueled up and going. (Beth thought the grease would keep us going.) About the best thing that can be said for boat food (after the fresh stuff is gone,) is that it squelches the appetite without leaving you with that "too full" feeling.

We had our evening tot of rum as the sun set. As a special treat Beth produced part of a slightly melted chocolate bar.

"You know, I never would have thought of having rum and chocolate back home but they're good together," Beth commented.

"Yeah, kind of like bananas and peanut butter, who would of thought they would go together."

"Hmmm, I wonder if they would back home."

"Gosh I wonder what's going on back there? How long have we been gone?"

"Oh....a little over two months."

"Is that all? So much has happened it seems a lot longer. I wonder what we've missed."

"Oh, probably a lot of rain...and, if we can believe Bully, an interesting time; compliments of the EPA."

"Hmmm. I wonder where he is. Do you think he's finally given up?"

"Now *that's* a good question. One that my Dad would have called, The Sixty-four Thousand Dollar Question."

Beth giggled into her mug. "I haven't heard that expression in forever."

"I guess it's been awhile. So, do you think the show was rigged?"

"What?"

"Don't you remember, they had to take it off the air because there was a scandal about it being rigged? They gave some of the contestants the answers. You know, like: How many offspring does the female chinchilla have during its life time?"

"Wild or tame?"

"See? Now if you had been the picked to be the winner of, The Sixty-four Thousand Dollar Question, you wouldn't have had to ask that dumb question."

"Why not? It's not a dumb question. It probably makes a lot of difference."

"True, but they would have given you both answers."

"Ah yes. I'm getting the picture, it was a little snowy at first. I'm afraid this was all before my time. All I got was the left-over cliche." She paused, took a sip of her rum, and then suddenly said, "Do you believe it? We've gone all this time, over two months, without watching T.V.? This is like a record for me. I've never gone over two days without watching T.V. in my whole life. I'll bet I even listened to it in the womb."

We went on talking about related things until our rum and chocolate was gone. Then Beth turned in.

I went on thinking of random things, and then I lit a rare cigar that I had picked up in Rangiroa. I used to smoke one every night, that or a pipe, but I quit the habit. I still like one occasionally. I guess all the talk of old stuff brought up an old craving. That's OK, my mouth will taste bad enough in the morning not to get the habit back.

Pacific Gold

The moon is rising later now and waning. No palm-fall moon this time. It seemed very dark. Bully and the phantom sailboat came into my mind. Would I see it tonight. I kept scanning the horizon. I didn't think they'd be using their nav lights; especially if it was Bully.

I started getting an ominous feeling. I checked the rigging with a flash-light; then walked around the boat looking at everything (I even clipped on my life-line.) But I didn't see anything unusual or suspicious. I felt like a submarine was about to surface next to us, or maybe Jaws, or old Moby Dick.

I tried to shrug off the feeling as the affects of the evening. Maybe rum and chocolate wasn't such a good idea--or maybe rum and chocolate *and* a cigar! Now that was possible. Especially after a dried and reconstituted supper. I tossed the cigar butt over the side and went back to the cockpit.

I almost sat back down when I thought, "Maybe I should take a look at the chart." Happy thought.

I went below very carefully and quietly so as not to wake the First Mate before her watch. I unrolled the chart holding the flashlight in my mouth and plotted out our present position by dead reckoning. And Bang! Right dead in the middle of our course, about a quarter of an inch from where I thought we were, was the symbol of a sunken ship!

"Arrgh, and what the hell is this?" I muttered, nearly dropping the flashlight.

Here we were, at least twenty miles from the nearest reef on the chart, and they stuck in a sunken ship symbol--actually a *half*-sunken ship symbol. This is the symbol that shows a ship half out of the water, indicating that it's not *totally* sunk--just wrecked. Like maybe it's sitting on a reef?

Did the cartographer just have an extra symbol lying around? Maybe he had a quota to fill? Or perhaps he thought he'd surprise someone reading his chart on a dark night in the midst of, *The Dangerous Archipelago*.

I quickly scanned the rest of the chart and found one more. But that one was on a definite reef on the south side of Rangiroa. I studied our little area of the chart again. It was there alright, and our course line was headed right for it. Not a little bit to one side or the other; no, right for it. Nothing else for miles around. "Jeez!"

All right! No point in running over the one possible hazard for miles around. Time to tack.

I checked to see that Beth wouldn't fall out of bed when we heeled the other direction, snapped off the light, and went back out into the cockpit.

The moon was just up and shining a path across the water towards us, but it wasn't showing anything else, like a wrecked ship or a reef dead ahead. But, what the hell, we had to go farther east anyway.

I readied the genoa sheets and pushed the tiller over. Helms-a-lee. Tack Ho. Etcetera. The mizzen and main booms swung across. I sheeted in the genoa and retied the tiller. A few things rattled around as they sought new positions below, and that was it.

I hate to admit it, but immediately I felt better. It must have been because the moon is up and it's not so dark. Had to be!

Pacific Gold

• *1200 5 December   Pos: S15°11', W144°28'*
Crs: 135°   Spd: 3 knts   Dpth: O.S.
Helmsman: Hispaniola
Comments: The last lap! Next stop: the Sea Gull Islands!

Hispaniola likes going to weather. With her sails trimmed I don't even need to set the wind vane. I just tie the tiller a little to windward and away she goes. She picks her own best slant and sticks to it. Beth says, the boat smells treasure and is as eager as we are. Maybe *Hispaniola* is a good name after all.

"I saw the boat," Beth announced when I relieved her at four. "This time it didn't have it's lights on. Do you want to eat now or wait a few hours?" She asked from the companionway.

"Now would be good."

"Great! I'm famished. I seem to get really hungry on watch just before sunrise. Like right now."

"Do you get hungry at this time when you're not on watch?"

She struck one of the big wooden kitchen matches, lit the stove, and then tossed the match over the side. "Could be. I don't know as I'm usually asleep."

"Next time I'll wake you and ask if you're hungry."

"No, that's alright." She was pumping water into a sauce pan with the foot pump. "You *have* awakened me and I *was* hungry." She put the pan on the burner and measured out a cup of rolled barley.

"So, what kind of a boat was it that you saw last night?"

"You're thinking I make these boats up, aren't you?"

"No. Not at all. I saw the one before this...or

are you?"

"Hmmm, that's right, you did. But if I know you, you thought I saw a dream boat." She poured the barley flakes into the boiling water and adjusted the flame on the burner. "It was kind of funny. You know how sometimes when a wave breaks it will look like a sail? Well, that's what I thought this was; a breaking wave. But it stayed there. I couldn't see it very well. It was nearly out of sight, but there was just enough moonlight for me to be sure that it was a sail. So I turned on the nav lights to see if it would answer. It disappeared. Over the horizon I guess. Or maybe our nav lights wrecked my night vision?"

Or maybe our lights scared them off? I thought, but said, "Could be I guess. I can see better with the lights off."

"It's kind of odd though; don't you think? I mean, all of these boat sightings at night, and always so far out that they disappear shortly after we see them?"

"Yes. It's almost as if someone is shadowing us, but how could they be doing that? They can't see us any better than we can see them. It would be awfully hard to predict when we are going to tack; especially last night."

"Unless they know where we are headed and they happen to be going to the same place. Maybe someone from the bar?"

"Who? The professor? Apparently he was the only one who had any idea about the Sea Gull Islands. Or was Bully there and we just didn't see him? Maybe he was in disguise?"

"Impossible."

I had to agree. "Well, maybe we'll find out tomorrow. Maybe someone will be at *Treasure Island* waiting."

"And if there is?"

"I don't know, maybe we'll just keep going and come back later. We could go on to Tahiti for a bit."

"What about other people? You know, the islanders that live there?"

"Ah, the locals, the natives, the Polynesians. Yes, that is a question."

"Well, what about them? Are we going to be able to just take our shovel and start digging up their airstrip without them wondering what's up?"

"Good question. According to the *Sailing Directions*, there aren't supposed to be any permanent residents. Just occasional visitors from the other islands that come to fish or make copra. If there are, I guess we'll play it by ear. Maybe we can share."

"Maybe. I don't know which option I like better; making a deal with the locals; or having a island deserted with an unknown sailboat shadowing us." Beth shivered.

"Yeah, I know what you mean. Guess we'll know more tomorrow."

• *1200 6 December   Pos: Tuanake Atoll of the Sea Gull Islands!*
Crs: N/A   Spd: 0 knts
Dpth: 25' anchored in the sand
Helmsman: none
Comments: Here at last!

Here at last! The largest island of the Sea Gull Islands, *Tuankee Atoll*. It isn't a very big atoll at that. The whole thing is maybe three miles wide and four long. There are two longish islands and a few little motus scattered around perimeter of the lagoon. It should be pretty easy to find the airstrip, if it's here. If not, there are only two other atolls, and they are even smaller. No sign of people of any kind so far.

The had wind picked up a little and remained steady for the last leg of the voyage. Not even any squalls. No phantom sailboats either. Just smooth sailing.

We were both pretty keyed up as it grew darker. I was smoking another rare cigar with my rum. Beth was having the last of the chocolate bar with hers.

"Here's to the last night of a long voyage." Beth raised her mug.

"Santé." I touched mine to hers with a clink and sipped a little rum. "And to *The Good Ship Hispaniola*, who carried us safely here."

"And, may she carry us safely away," Beth added as we clinked and drank again.

We both stayed on watch, watching for the mystery boat. Finally I turned in about eleven. "Wake me if you see any boats."

"OK. What will we do if it shows up? Sail towards it?"

"That's an idea. Or maybe we could just heave-to and let it catch up? I don't know. Here," I handed her the hand compass from below. "Get a bearing if you see it."

"Good idea," she agreed. "Well, night-night Captain Jack--don't forget, *Treasure Island* tomorrow."

"Thanks for reminding me, now I'm supposed to sleep?"

"I won't be able to, why should you?"

But I did, and she did in her turn. And the hand compass remained unused. Maybe we had tacked once too often for the company to stay with us. Or maybe there really were a few boats around going about their own businesses. Or maybe we had been at sea too long and imagined the whole thing.

At any rate the sun came up on schedule.

Pacific Gold

About ten AM *Katiu Atoll* came abeam to starboard and we spotted *Tuanake Atoll* shortly after. Going through the pass was a breath-holder because the chart didn't give any depths and it looked shallow. I was up on the spreaders so I could see the coral heads better as we squeaked through. The sun was high overhead and the view was great--especially when we were safely into the lagoon.

I navigated us over a patch of sand, near the largest islet, to drop anchor.

CHAPTER 14: In The Sea Gulls

* *0800, December 11 Pos: Tuanake Atoll*
Crs: none Spd: 0   Dpth: 4 fathoms
Helmsman: 25lb Danforth
Comments: Feels like home.

Back at *Tuanake*. Beautiful atoll. Maybe we should just stay here the rest of our lives. The sun is hot, the sand white, the water calm and blue, palm trees gently swaying in the trade winds; marvelous.

We sailed to *Tepoto Atoll* after a quick survey of *Tuanake*. It is slightly smaller and just as beautiful.

Unfortunately neither atoll seems to have the least trace of an emergency landing strip. That left *Hiti Atoll* which is very small. I think it's an unlikely spot for an emergency air strip since you can't get into the lagoon and it's so small. It seems like there are a lot of better

Pacific Gold

places around--but then, what do I know?

So, we had to check out *Hiti*.

"How are we going to do that?" Beth asked.

"Another sixty-four thousand dollar question. There is no pass into the lagoon. The water is much to deep to anchor outside. And it's eighteen and a half miles from *Tuanake*--so it would be a tough row in the dinghy..."

"...And then we would still have to get over the reef somehow." Beth finished for me. "Nobody said this treasure hunting would be easy, but this just took a big leap in the difficult direction."

"Well, let's go take a look at it," I suggested. "Maybe the book is being pessimistic."

Beth shrugged, "Looking sounds good to me Captain, as long as we're careful about it."

"Aye!"

We pulled the anchor and slipped out *Tepoto's* placid lagoon. After tacking over to *Hiti*, we slowly circumnavigated the atoll. Studying the shoreline and reef intently, we saw a house. Probably just a temporary place as the *Sailing Directions* said there are no permanent residents. We didn't see a good way to get ashore (or anything that looked like an old abandoned emergency landing strip either.)

So, we sailed back to *Tuanake* and anchored in our old spot. (Just like we live here.)

The next morning I rowed ashore to walk around and think. Maybe I'd stumble across a clue to our mystery. I still believed that this was our island. Our *Treasure Island*.

Why anyone in their right minds would pick it over some of the other atolls, like *Rangiroa* (even if the hotel and topless women weren't there then,) eluded me. But it doesn't do any good to question *military intelligence*. Maybe they were looking for the most unlikely location; isolated, unpopulated, and hard to get into to. In that case *Hiti* would fill the bill just fine. Which also, incidentally, might make it the best place for a pirate to bury a treasure.

The more I thought about it, the more I convinced myself that there was a certain logic for *Hiti* to be our *Treasure Island*, but how to check it out? It would have been relatively easy for the pirates or the military. They could have left part of the crew on the ship to sail it around while a small party made it over the reef in a whale boat. Maybe they did find a small passage into the lagoon? Or they may have commuted by small boat from *Tuanake*. We could do the same thing. Beth could sail Hispaniola while I rowed ashore, as long as nothing went wrong. Like me flipping the dinghy in the surf and damaging myself.

I had a feeling it would be hard to sell Beth on that plan, I was having trouble buying it myself. But...could we row over? Eighteen and a half miles, rowing at one to two knots, would take twelve--fourteen hours.?? A very long open ocean row in a eight foot pram. That's not even thinking about random currents and being out of sight of land--navigating. The old Polynesians would think nothing of doing it, but for us...well, there would be a high panic quotient. Damn, a good sailing dinghy would come in handy here. But then we'd still have to make a surf landing over the reef. Well, that might not be so bad in a boat that draws six inches (or less) of water. Maybe we could find a place to sneak over the reef if we could get there. Could I rig a sail and a dagger board on the dinghy? Hmmm......

I looked out at *Hispaniola* in time to see a naked Beth dive over board. OK, enough of this serious left brain thought. Turning the matter over to my subconscious I rowed out to the sailboat for a swim--or maybe, a beer.

I lounged in the cockpit with a warm beer while Beth complacently soaked in the tepid lagoon. Her long, sun bleached blond hair resembled a halo as it floated around her head. Her nose, lips, and closed eyes were just above the water's surface. The soft, well tanned shoulders--barely awash. Her breasts floated like little tropical islands; each with a brown volcanic peak abruptly rising from a gently sloping white beach. Farther south, a slight mound formed an atoll. The belly-button lagoon was complete with small hip bone motus--there was even a bit of foliage on the south shore. A leisurely kick caused a tsunami to sweep across the whole tantalizing archipelago. Just like what could have wiped out Uncle Carlyle's airstrip.

Lying in the shade of the cockpit awning and sipping warm beer, it occurred to me that perhaps the gold was unimportant. Maybe *this* was treasure enough. What could heaven offer that would be better?

Pondering this major question, I tilted my head back to take another sip from the beer bottle and saw a sailboat entering the pass.

"Arrgh," I said, choking on my beer.

My coughing and spluttering disturbed Beth's equilibrium, her seductive islands and peaks disappeared as her head emerged. "You OK?"

Coughing, I pointed toward the pass.

"Oh shit." She swam to the ladder and climbed aboard grabbing a towel from the lifeline enroute. She quickly wrapped it around her. "Who do you think it is?"

For some reason, though I can't say why, the boat had an ominous appearance. It was just another thirty-five or forty foot black, fiberglass sailboat--but this one looked threatening. "Hard telling. Maybe it's our mystery boat." We hadn't seen or mentioned it since we'd gotten to the Sea Gull Islands and I'd forgotten to worry about it.

"I don't like it," Beth said from below where she was getting dressed.

"Nor I. But, I don't think I'd like any boat that dared to alter our solitary tranquility."

"Perhaps not," she agreed as she rejoined me in the cockpit. The boat came closer. "No, I just don't like *that* boat."

"I have to agree with you." (Maybe it was the searching radar antenna mounted on a pedestal above the transom.)

Our suspicions were confirmed a moment later when Bully sauntered up to the boats bow pulpit and hollered, "Hi y'all. No need to get all dressed up. It's just your ol' pal, the Bull, and a couple of friends come to visit. Hee hee hee!"

The black boat motored uncomfortably close and Bully let the anchor splash into the lagoon. The boat's sails hung limply as the chain ran out and formed a big pile on top of the anchor. "Dang," Bully commented after he finally got the exiting chain stopped. "That sucker really takes off."

In the quiet that followed I recognized the person at the helm as the solitary drinker in the hotel bar at *Rangiroa*. The dark little man wearing a beat up jungle hat, a ratty (army issue) olive drab green tee shirt, and camouflage fatigue pants came forward along the near rail.

"This is my buddy, Grunt. You should get to know each, Jack. Grunt's an old war hero too. That's where he got the name. Hee hee hee."

"Shut up Ass Hole, and get the sails down," Grunt growled. Bully stifled his snickering.

Pacific Gold

At this point the lady with the Scandinavian accent and long nails (also from the hotel bar,) appeared in the cockpit. "And this is Christina," Bully said with a grandiose wave of his hand. He released the jib halyard and the sail fell mostly onto the foredeck.

Christina stared vacantly.

"So, Chilluns--how's things?" Bully smirked with a giant wink. "Y'all been doin' any good diggin' lately?" He uncleated the main halyard. The boom fell into the gallows with a thud and the rust stained main sail rattled down. The two men wadded it up on the boom and restrained it with a couple of black rubber bungees.

"At least you get right to the point." Beth observed.

"Yup, no more pussy footin'. I tried ta be nicey nicey, and what'd it get me? Nothin' but rudeness. I jus' wanted ta hep ya out, but ya jus give me a bad time so....I met up with ol' Grunt here an was talkin' 'bout treasure huntin' an all. An' he allowed as how it's a dangerous business for beginners. So we jus' mosey'd on down ta make sure ya all was okey dokey."

"Well, *us* all are okey dokey so why don't *you* all just mosey on out of here and leave *us* all alone?" Beth replied.

Bully slapped his forehead with the palm of his hand. "If thet don' beat all." He turned to Grunt. "Ya see what I've been up against? Nuthin' but ungrateful rudeness."

"Yeah," Beth interrupted his theatrics. "So why don't you take the hint and leave us alone?"

"Alright! Knock it off!" Grunt interjected impatiently. "I didn't spend a week beating down here to listen to you butt heads diddle-fart around. Cut to the stash." He turned to Bully. "Go aboard and haul out the bloody treasure."

"Over my dead body! Nobody's boarding this boat without a fight." Beth declared.

Grunt appraised her through cold eyes, "Don't tempt me sugar. I'm sure the sharks would like a little white meat for a change." He turned back to Bully, "Move, Shit-head."

Bully hesitated, glowered at the dark man, then reached down and picked up a long handled boat hook from the deck. "Ok, ok...what's the danged hurry," he muttered.

I put my hand on Beth's shoulder and said, "Come on, let's go forward. The air is fresher and the view better."

She turned to me with tears of anger in her eyes, "But... but... we can't just let them onto our boat. They don't have the right to..to..."

"Anything." I finished for her. "I know Honey," I urged her gently forward. "I know, but there isn't any treasure. And it isn't worth fighting about--at the moment."

"No treasure?" Bully had pulled the boats together and was about to step on board, now he hesitated. "What do you mean no treasure? Didn't you find it on that other island?"

"Nope."

"Why...why not?"

"Didn't find anything. Hey, you want my shovel? Go dig to your hearts content. I couldn't find anything."

"Well, why'd you come back then? Why aren't you still over there diggin'?"

"Got tired." I shrugged my shoulders and sat down on the cabin roof beside Beth.

"God-dammit! Will you get your dead ass over there and scout out that stash? Bleedin' jar-head marines never were worth a shit without a boot up their butts. Move dammit!" Grunt yelled at Bully like a drill Sargent.

Bully moved. He put one foot onto

Hispaniola. Then he stopped and twisted around. "You watch your foul mouth little man." he said angrily. "I'm the one who found this treasure, not you." He gestured towards Grunt with the boat hook. "I'll go aboard and get it when I'm good and ready! Until then pipe down or I'll shove this hook up your aaaa..." Since he was no longer holding the two boats together, they drifted apart dumping Bully into the lagoon.

Beth and I peered over the side. Bully's dirty yellow "Cat" hat floated near the boat hook. He surfaced a short distance away snorting, coughing, and blowing, and shouting. "Hep! Hep me!" (cough, cough) "Hep! I'm gonna drown!!" Which was true--Bully obviously hadn't taken any red-cross swimming lessons lately.

"Do something!" Beth demanded indignantly of Grunt.

Grunt casually watched Bully floundering. "Sink or swim Butt-head."

"What!" she screamed.

Grunt smiled evilly. "One less to share with."

Bully was obviously loosing the battle.

"Over here! Bully! Over here!" Beth shouted.

Bully paddled wildly and actually made some headway towards our boarding ladder.

I grabbed the boat hook out of the water and extended it towards him. "Here bully, Grab hold."

"Let him be!" Grunt said. "Sharks'll take care of his lard ass."

Bully grabbed hold of the hook. With a wild look in his eyes he looked frantically around for sharks.

"Easy Bull--easy," I counseled tugging him

towards the boarding ladder. "Don't worry about sharks, they don't want you."

Bully lunged to the ladder. Coughing and sputtering he pulled himself on board. He slumped down on the cabin roof with water draining form his clothes.

"Why Bully, you're getting bald," Beth said, in an astonished tone of voice as she eyed a dead white patch of skin to the back of Bully's head.

"Oh God, my cap!" he responded slapping the bald spot. "I'll get sun burn."

I looked over to where it floated between the boats. "I'll get it." Beth and I went forward with the boathook.

"Jeez, look at the oil slick on the water that's around it. I think it's hazardous waste." Beth observed.

I hauled it in and extended it on the end of the hook to Bully. He grabbed it and slapped it onto his head. He looked like Bully, again. A sodden, discouraged Bully, but still Bully.

Grunt was frenetically pacing the decks of his boat like a mad man. "All right!" he hollared. "All right! Quit screwing around and get to it! Let's get this operation over with!"

Bully sat on the cabin roof, his head hung down dejectedly. In response to Grunt's urging, he swiveled around and peered down the companionway. "Damn," he said. "Jack, this'd be a whole lot easier if you'd just co-operate and share with us. We'll be fair about it."

Yeah right, I thought. And what is your fair share? Zero. But it really didn't matter. We didn't have any treasure to share. "Bully, there is no treasure on this boat. There is nothing to share (fairly or otherwise.)"

"Will you get your dead ass down below and rip that boat apart and find that bleeding treasure? Or do I have to come over and show

Pacific Gold

you how?" Grunt yelled.

"Jack says there ain't no treasure."

"What the hell did you think he'd say? Jeez!" Grunt kicked the cap rail of his boat in disgust and I noticed that he wasn't barefoot like most tropical sailors. He was wearing jungle boots. I hadn't seen any of them since Viet Nam. Actually, he looked like an advertisement for an Army Surplus store. He even had used hand grenade pins stuck in his hat. The only things missing were his dog-tags slung around his neck.

Bully's face was getting redder than normal, I could see a little vein throbbing in the side of his head.

"Where are your dog-tags soldier!" I demanded of Grunt.

"What?" Grunt's hand went to his throat.

"Your dog-tags. It looks like you've got everything else."

"Your damn right I do. I've even got a string of gook ears below. Had to put them in a jar of alcohol 'cause they started to stink too much." He laughed a little crazily. "Don't need no damn dog-tags. I'm a free agent now." He shook his head defiantly and stomped across the deck.

Yup, I thought, he's certifiable. Good job Bully, way to pick your associates.

Bully stood uncertainly in the companionway. "It's true, I seen 'em. Looks like a jar of pickled onion rings on a string. The guy's a little nuts." Shaking his head he peered reluctantly below.

"Go on down," I quietly urged him, "Take a look. You won't find anything because there isn't anything *too* find. Just don't tear things up, OK?"

"Right." he agreed sullenly.

"Don't tear things up!" Grunt exploded. "What the hell do think pirates do? Damn chicken shit crews a man has to put up with!" He stormed back to the cockpit of his boat. Christina was standing uncertainly to one side-- but not far enough. "Out of my way Bitch!" he yelled, slapping her aside before going below.

She squeaked and said, "David please stop."

Oh brother, I thought as I listened to him thumping and banging around in the other boat, and wasn't the least surprised when he emerged brandishing an AK-47 rifle, complete with the largest banana clip in the world.

Holding the rifle in one hand he fired a short burst into the sky. "Alright now! Let's have some action. Everybody on deck!" Bully was standing in the companionway with just his head head poking out of the main hatch way. "Now!" Grunt pointed the rifle at Bully's head.

"Awright, awright," Bully mumbled as he clambered on deck. "Jeez fella, simmer down, simmer down will ya?"

"I'll simmer down when I get some action. Do you think I brought you down here for a picnic? Tie those two up!" He ordered waving the automatic rifle in our direction. I involuntarily winced. It's so easy to fire off a few rounds while waving an automatic rifle around with your finger on the trigger.

"Wuh why," Bully stammered. "They aren't doing anything."

"Because *I'm* coming over there and *I* want them tied up! *That's* why. Understand?" Grunt punctuated his speech by wildly gesturing with the AK.

"OK, OK, calm down will ya? You're makin' me nervous wavin' that gun around like that!"

"Listen Shit-head, clean out your

Pacific Gold

cauliflower ears and listen. Number one: this is not a gun! This is a rifle! Number two: nobody tells Grunt what or what not to do? If you don't like what Grunt do, jump over the side again. Understand?" He grinned wolfishly and gestured over the side with the rifle.

In some corner of my mind I wondered if he would have liked for Bully to try to get away so he could shoot a swimming target and watch the sharks clean up the evidence.

"OK, OK," Bully grabbed the coiled up genoa sheet off a cleat on the mizzen mast. "I said OK, didn't I?" He tossed the words back over his shoulder as he shambled forward towards where we were sitting on the cabin roof.

"Tie them to the mast!"

"Oh brother!" Bully mumbled. "Come on-- you heard him. Don't make this difficult. Stand up by the mast."

We stood up, one on either side of the mast. "Bully, don't do this," Beth pleaded.

"I'm sorry, I got to. He's got that gun."

"Jack...." Beth sobbed. I could feel her quivering on the other side of the mast. "....I don't like this."

"Hey, knock off the chatter," Grunt yelled. "And make them face each other. Yeah, turn them around! I want them to be able to watch what happens to each other. Hee Hee Hee." He laughed in fiendish anticipation of whatever he was thinking of doing.

Bully tied a bowline around my left wrist. Beth was whimpering. He stopped and looked at her. "Naw, I ain't gonna do this," he muttered and threw the rope down on the deck. "The heck with this," he said to Grunt. "They don't need to be tied up."

Grunt looked like he was about to explode, waving the rifle around erratically he screamed, "What do you mean; don't need to be! *I* want them tied up! Who's giving the orders around here anyway? Not you Jar-head! No wonder you marines lost the friggin' war for us!"

Bully stiffened, put his hands on his hips. "Now wait just a pea-pickin' minute. Who put you in charge anyway? This was my idea. So back off!"

Grunt answered with his high pitched laugh. Pointing the AK-47 at Bully's gut, he said, "This puts me in charge, Buck Wheat. And I'm sick of screwin' with you. Get back up against that mast between them two."

Bully hesitated, his eyes fixed on the rifles muzzle. Grunt moved it a trifle to the side and squeezed off a round. The bullet smacked into the cabin wall. Bully jumped into place at the mast.

Somehow that made me feel better. Bully is an ass-hole, but he wasn't in Grunt's league. So now he was forced to be on our side--even if our side was about to be tied up.

"Wench!" Grunt roared as best as he could. "Get your ass over there and tie up those butt heads." Christina came sullenly forward. I saw that in addition to the fresh red splotch where he had just slapped her, she had older bruises including a black eye that was turning green. Another addition to our side, I thought. Even if she can't help us, she won't hurt us if she isn't forced to.

There was a small problem however. The boats were about six feet apart. Too far to step, or for Christina to jump, across. She walked up and stood dumbly at the rail. Grunt looked around his deck. He appeared baffled for a moment and then spied his boat hook on Hispaniola.

Pacific Gold

"Hey, gimme back my hook!"

"No." I responded.

"What do you mean, No? It's mine. Now hand it over."

"I found it floating in the water. How do I know it's yours? I don't see your name written on it."

Grunt appeared perplexed. He looked down, apparently saw the rifle hanging by his side and jerked it up. "Now Fart-face! Hand it over or I'll blast you where you stand."

"No you won't. I was a helicopter pilot in Nam; you were an infantryman. I may have saved your butt."

He glowered, he stomped one foot. He jerked the rifle around erratically. Then he said in a low voice. "*You* never saved *my* ass, Flyboy. Besides, that's all done with. It's over! Them politicians screwed us." He jerked the rifle back up. "So that don't count for nothin'. Move Dammit!"

"Shoot me and you'll never get the treasure."

"What do you mean? I can shoot everybody and just come over and grab it."

"No you can't, because it's not here. I told you. There is no buried treasure on this boat. I didn't find it. And I'm the one who knows where to look for it--it was *my* Uncle who found it here during World War Two. Let's deal."

Grunt squinted at me, lowered the rifle a bit, and for a moment I thought I'd gotten through to him. But then the two boats perversely drifted together with a dull "Thunk." Grunt jerked and said, "Awright." He prodded Christina with the rifle butt and followed her aboard Hispaniola.

Under Grunts supervision Christina tied us to the main mast; back to back now, Beth to starboard, Bully forward, and me to port. Basically she went round and round the mast (and us) until she used up all forty feet of the five eighths inch rope that was the genoa sheet. It took a long time, but in the process, by Grunts direction, I think she tied every hitch known to man--probably even the diamond hitch. When she finished we were firmly encased in rope from neck to waist.

When she ran out of rope, Grunt picked up the end of the jib sheet and said, "Alright Sweet Pea, your turn." He pushed Christina roughly back against Bully. "Since you two are starting to like each other so much, I'll just tie you together."

As he set to work, he giggled and said, "Just like a preacher I'll tie the knot." He giggled some more. "...'til death do you part."

Christina remained sullenly silent as Grunt put a couple of wraps of rope around her, fastening her to Bully. She was facing forward and, with Bully between her and the mast, she was nearly standing on the forward hatch cover which opened into the forepeak.

"There now, that's frickin'double-A better." He declared surveying his handiwork. "It's a sorry situation when a Captain can't trust his crew. But..." he shrugged elaborately and smirked.

He stopped in front of Beth. "Now don't you look pretty? Maybe you and me can negotiate something to our mutual benefit--later." He reached towards her, she flinched, he jerked back his hand. "Later," he scolded himself. " Business first, then we'll have some fun..."

Grunt stomped back to the cockpit and went below. We could hear him casually knocking things about. There was a crash of pots and pans. "Oops, sorry!" he called out, with that

Pacific Gold

high pitched giggle I was beginning to hate.
 "He's a ravin' lunatic." Bully whispered hoarsely.
 "He's an addict," Christina said quietly.
 "What?" Beth queried. "What kind of an addict?"
 "He's a drug addict. That boat's got any drug you can imagine on board."
 "So, he's not always like this?"
 "No," Bully interjected. "He seemed like a normal human bean before this. A little gloomy, but nothing like this. This guys berserk." Bully tried to gesture with his hands and the ropes nearly choked the rest of us.
 "Ouch," Christina said. "Try not to move around so, Billy. Yes, he's very erratic. It's the drugs."
 "So, how did you wind up with him?" Beth asked Christina.
 "I was in Jamaica and had to leave in a hurry. He offered me a way out and I took it. I figured it couldn't be as bad as a Jamaican jail."
 "But, why do you stay with him?" Beth asked.
 "I to leave my passport behind, I can't leave the boat until I get another one. We'd been on *Rarotonga* four months and I have been hoping that it would come on every mail plane--but not yet."
 "So how did you guys find us?" I asked.
 "That was easy, Grunt just asked the Professor which way you were going and then followed using the radar. We could stay just over the horizon and still see you with the radar. Sometimes we got a little closer, at night to check and make sure we were following the right boat. Of course he has night vision glasses."
 "Of course. So, Bernard just told him where

we were going?"

"I guess so, Grunt didn't take me with him. So maybe it wasn't that simple." Christina replied.

"He told me the old guys specs got broke," Bully said.

"Well, that was mean," Beth said. "Ouch, what are you doing Jack? Can't you stand still?"

"I'm trying to get my jack-knife out of my pocket so I can start cutting these ropes." I whispered.

"What for?" she whispered back. "It won't take him long to find out that there is no treasure onboard."

"Yeah, well, what then? You don't think he'll just untie us and go on his unmerry way do you?"

"No....I guess not. What do you think he'll do then?"

"Then, I think we'll find out just how mean the little son-of-a-bitch is. I've seen guys with ear collections before."

"Shush, he's in the forepeak," Beth whispered harshly.

We could hear him bumping around under our feet. Then it was quiet. "Now what's he doing?"

We waited, straining to hear. Suddenly the heavy teak hatch cover in front of Christina burst open and Grunts head popped up. "AArrggh!" He yelled and grabbed for Christina's legs.

Christina tried to jump out of the way and her feet landed on top of the hatchcover while her upper body remained tied to Bully and the mast. The heavy hatch cover slammed back down on Grunt's head and caught his arms outside.

Grunt howled and thrashed around trying

to free his arms but Christina bore down with all her weight and Bully joined in too. Their combined efforts caused the ropes to tighten unmercifully on Beth and me, but I urged them to keep him pinned.

"Don't let him out. Keep the pressure on."

After a few moments Grunt was quiet.

Beth moaned as the ropes cut into her.

"What is he doing now?" Christina asked.

"I don't know, but whatever it is he's not doing it with his hands."

"Hey," Grunt said from under the hatch cover. "Hey Christina. Come on let me out. I was just having some fun. Are you forgetting that I got you out of that jam in Jamaica? You owe me. If it wasn't for me you'd be rotting in jail--or worse."

"Yes, or I could be locked up on your boat waiting for you to hit me again. Sorry, I've already paid."

"Aw, it wasn't that bad. You liked it."

"I think you're sick."

"Everyone's a little sick." He pushed on the hatch cover with his head. Caught momentarily off guard the cover came up a bit, but Christina and Bully quickly forced it back down. Grunt's wrist's remained firmly trapped.

Meanwhile I was vainly trying to free us, but couldn't, there were just too many knots and hitches in too much rope. It was a stand off.

It got very quiet. The only sounds were the faint lapping of the water on the hull, the omnipresent sound of the surf crashing at regular intervals against the outside reef, the occasional cry of a sea bird, and our breathing. The sun was getting low in the sky. We were thirsty. I realized that I was feeling drowsy.

I forced my attention back to our plight. "Don't relax," I cautioned Christina and Bully.

"Don't let him surprise you."

"I'm gettin' tired of this," Bully said. "How long do we gotta stay like this?"

"Until something happens I guess."

"Like what?"

"I don't know, but whatever it is it should be better than him getting loose. If he gets loose we'll all suffer--a lot. I've got a feeling he'd enjoy torturing us."

"What do you mean?" a weak muffled voice came from from under the hatch cover. "You're torturing me. I can't even feel my hands anymore. This is needless. I was only fooling. I'm not going to hurt you. Come on, let me out." he whined.

"Hah! No way. Keep the pressure on Bully. Christina, you know what he can do--don't relax now." Beth responded.

"But, we can't stay this way forever. We got to do something, don't we?" Bully objected.

"Well, let's figure something out. We can't be turning him loose with us still tied up. That doesn't make sense."

"We have to do something, this rope is killing me." Beth said.

"I agree, but what?"

"Where's the ends to these damn ropes?"

We occupied ourselves for the next hour or so with trying to figure out just how we were tied with very little progress and there was still no getting the jack-knife out of my pocket.

Things were looking real bad as the sun slipped closer and closer to the western ocean. I didn't think we could hold out for long after dark.

That's when we began to hear whimpering coming from under the hatch cover. And then, "Come on guys, let me out. You don't have to be afraid of me. You're killing me. I, I need some medicine. I need it real bad....I've got a stash; I'll share." The voice was very weak and desperate sounding. Almost like a small boy.

I turned my head toward Christina. "Medicine? What kind of medicine? Is he diabetic or something?"

"No, I told you; he's an addict. He needs a fix."

"Oh great, you mean he's crashing."

"Yes."

"Eeeyahh!" He screamed and started butting his head against the hatch cover. The hatch cover bucked up and down, but not enough for him to get free. He screamed again.

"God, I don't think I can take much more of this," Bully said. "It's like I can feel his arms crushing every time the hatch cover goes back down."

"You can take it," I urged. "Just think what he'll do if you let him loose."

Grunt quieted down again and all we could hear was a muffled mumbling or sobbing.

Twilight was coming on fast when I heard, *"Bonjour."*

I jerked in surprise and banged my head against the mast. There in front of me was a Polynesian outrigger canoe with a very old man and a small girl in it.

Christina recovered from her surprise first and responded, *"Bonjour Monsieur."*

"Madame. Comment ally vous?"

Christina proceeded to *comment* in rapid French about our situation.

"Mais oui Madam." The old man paddled to the swim ladder and climbed spryly onboard.

"What did you say?" Beth asked eagerly.

"I told him we were being held by a crazy man and asked him to please untie us."

The old man looked cautiously below first.

We heard a sobbing snarl from Grunt. Then the old man came forward. The little girl, who looked to be about eight years old, remained in the canoe and, at his direction, paddled out a bit from *Hispaniola*.

He surveyed the situation a moment or two, then muttered, "Yes, yes." It took him about a half an hour to untie all the knots and hitches that held us.

Unfortunately, towards the end of the process, Bully and Christina took their weight off the hatch-cover enough for Grunt to jerk his hands free.

Fortunately, after having the circulation cut off from them for several hours he couldn't use them for much. But he roared and raged and came out from below like a wild animal cradling the AK-47 rifle in his arms. He bellowed incoherently with spit drooling from his mouth. I jerked free of the last ropes and we stood bunched on the foredeck.

"Jeez! Now what?" Bully asked as Grunt came menacingly forward.

"Grab the rifle--before he can use it!" Beth shouted.

Grunt was fumbling for the trigger with fingers that wouldn't work. Bully lurched forward and wrenched the rifle out of Grunts hands. As he did one of Grunt's fingers snagged the trigger and the rifle came to life spitting lead. Everyone on the foredeck, including the old man, dove over the side. I surfaced in time to see the end of a brief struggle in which Grunt was knocked off the boat.

The little girl picked up the old man in the canoe. As I swam to Hispaniola's swim ladder, I noticed that the name on the transom of the big boat was *Marauder*. Now that's a fitting name, I thought as we straggled up Hispaniola's swim

Pacific Gold

ladder; all except for Grunt that is. He had disappeared in the dark lagoon.

"Where did he go?" Beth put everyone's question into words. "Did he sneak back onto his own boat?"

I didn't want to go looking, but we had to know that he wasn't getting ready for another attack. Reluctantly, I pulled the two boats boats together. "Come on Bully, we'd better check it out."

We stepped lightly onto the foredeck and then proceeded down opposite sides of the bigger boat to the cockpit. It was tense, but it didn't take long to determine that Grunt wasn't onboard.

We tied the two boats together so it would be easier to watch both. I *really* didn't want to be surprised by Grunt. When we were done, the old man and little girl came on board, Beth got out the rum bottle, and we sat around the cockpit of the bigger boat.

"You speak some english?" I asked the old man.

He nodded. *"Oui, petit."*

"This is Bully, Christina, Beth, and I'm Jack," I introduced us extending my hand.

He took my hand and shook it saying, "I am pleased to meet you. I am called *Pupure,* and this is *Nga*." He put his arm around the little girl who snuggled close to his side. "Grand daughter."

He spoke his english carefully and it was clear that he wasn't used to it, but he spoke with a familiar accent. "Are you American?"

He thought about it before he replied. "Once, yes. Now Tuamotan." He paused and then asked, "Why you come here?"

"We were looking for buried treasure." Beth answered gaily. I think we were all a little giddy after our rescue. And the rum was rapidly adding to it.

The old man hesitated. I thought maybe he was having trouble translating, but then he asked Beth, "Why you think there is treasure buried here?"

Beth looked at me, I shrugged my shoulders. I'd kind of lost interest in the whole project. "Jack's Uncle was here during World War Two. He wrote to Jack's Grandmother that there was some gold buried here; so, we thought we'd take a look."

The old man turned to me, "What surname?"

"Astor, John J. Astor is my full name."

The old man nodded slowly. "Your Father's name?"

"Sam, he died a few years ago."

The old man was silent for a long while, slowly nodding. Finally he said, "Guess I'm the Uncle."

CHAPTER 15: A Whole 'Nother Branch of the Family!

- *1800 December 21 Pos: Hiti lagoon*
Crs: Steady as she goes! Spd:N.A.
Dpth: @ anchor in 3 fathoms
Helmsperson: Carlyle
Comments: How about that?

Uncle Carlyle's pronouncement was followed by a very long, deep silence.

Stunned silence, on my part.

So my long, dead/lost, missing-in-action, Uncle Carlyle was not only not killed in the war, but was, incredibly, still alive. And, though arguably missing, was alive here, here where his letter said he had found enough gold for the rest of his life. Suddenly the pieces fell into place. A real head slapper. He disappeared and came here, dug up his gold, and....lived. Lived the life he chose. It was true that he looked old and used. Very few teeth left, thin scraggly long gray hair, skin brown and wrinkled like old leather--but he really was old. He had to be at least seventy-five or eighty. He was alive, and looked--if not happy; contented. Even now when suddenly confronted by a nephew that he'd probably never heard of and certainly never expected to meet, he didn't appear to be off balance.

"Did you think someone would come looking for you? I mean one of us; a relative?"

He looked up slowly and took his time replying, "I don't know. Maybe at first, but the war was on. No I guess not. Not really."

I waited, but that was all. There was just the quiet lapping of wavelets on the hull and the subdued roar of the surf on the outer reef.

"So why did you come by today?" Beth asked. "Did you just happen by or...?"

"Oh, I saw you circle *Hiti* a couple of days ago. So I thought I'd come over and see if you were here. Sometimes I like a little conversation about the outside world."

"Do you live on *Hiti*?"

Uncle Carlyle nodded his head, "*Oui*. What brings you here? Oh, that's right, you said you were looking for treasure. Why is that?"

I explained about finding the letters and reading his about the treasure.

He took that in for awhile and finally replied. "So they're both dead then?"

"Yes, their bundles of letters ended with a letter from the government saying they were killed in action, but yours said, '*Missing in action.*'"

He chuckled a little. "Yes, I went missing."

"How did that happen?"

"Well, it was nearly accidental. I had worked my way across the Pacific with the

Pacific Gold

seabees building things. And it wasn't a bad life. We got to see a lot of nice places. But that changed in the Phillipines. The Japanese were there and there was a lot of hard fighting. It was exciting at first, but I didn't care for it. Then I got sick and they put me in sick bay. (I was hoping they would send me home.) Then, just as I was getting released from the hospital, the Japanese kicked us out of the those islands. Which was fine with me--MacArthur, he vowed to go back, but not many of us felt that way." He took another slug of his rum and settled back a little more comfortably. "So, who's who here?"

"Beth and I are on that boat, Hispaniola, and we were looking for the treasure that you mentioned in your letter. Bully and Christina, along with Grunt, were looking for us hoping to cut in on the treasure."

Uncle Carlyle nodded.

"So how did you get to be missing?" Beth asked.

He took another thoughtful drink and then said, "Well, I was just out of sick bay and on my way to rejoin my unit when, suddenly we had to get out of the Phillipines. Mass confusion. I was at the airport looking for a ride to where my unit was supposed to be: Truk island or someplace like that. When a Sargent came running up and asked if I was going to Tahiti. Without even thinking I said, Yes. He said I'd better hurry. So I grabbed my sea-bag, ran over and boarded the airplane. From Tahiti it was pretty easy to get out here to the Tuamotus. And I've been pretty much here, ever since. At first I thought a lot about going back home--but I was a deserter, so I steered clear of anything American for awhile. I guess it doesn't matter much anymore, but now I have no desire to go where it is cold and....and it's really nice here."

"So, did you find the treasure?" Bully cut in. He'd been quiet until then, but now he couldn't restrain himself.

Uncle Carlyle considered Bully for a moment before answering. "Yes. I dug it up. When the war was over I went to Europe and sold the gold. I spent some of the money looking around there. But I soon realized that this was where I wanted to be."

"So now you live on *Hiti*?" Beth asked.

Uncle Carlyle smiled, "Yes, I married a woman who's family owns *Hiti*--so we decided to live here."

"By yourselves?"

"The rest of the family comes and goes, but Raua and I stay most of the time. There is really no reason to leave, except, now and then I get to wanting to see some of my own kind of people. So, occasionally a sailboat stops here or at *Tepoto* and I go visiting. Once in a while we go to *Rangiroa* or *Tahiti*."

He asked about the family back in Oregon. We told him about the old house falling into the ocean and other things we could think of.

Finally we finished our cups of rum. Decided on a watch schedule, and turned in. Bully and Christina would sleep on the big boat, Beth and I on Hispaniola, Uncle Carlyle and his grand daughter, Nga, slept on deck. I think he would have preferred going ashore, but not with the possibility of a crazy man prowling about. I'm sure Grunt's location was at the top of everyone's top ten question list, but we heard no more from him.

"Now what?" Bully asked the next morning. I shrugged my shoulders. We Astors were finishing our breakfasts in Hispaniola's cockpit. (Bully and Christina were on the other boat.)

Uncle Carlyle licked some syrup from his scraggly mustache, cleared his throat and said, "I'd like you and Beth to come over to *Hiti* and meet the rest of my family, if you have the time. Raua has so many relatives, it would be fun to introduce her to couple of mine."

I looked at Beth, she nodded energetically.

"Is there a pass we can get through with *Hispaniola*?" I asked, patting the deck.

"How much water do you draw?"

"Five and a half feet."

"I can guide you in at high tide."

"That will be after dark."

"No problem."

"All right. Lets go!"

I got up handing my plate to Beth and went over to the rail where I began untying the the line that held the two boats together.

"Hey! What about us?" Bully demanded.

"What about you?"

"What are we going to do? And what about Grunt? What if he comes back?"

I continued untying the boats. "I guess you guys will just have to figure it out for yourselves."

"Hey, wait just a pea-pickin' minute. Don't be forgettin' I took that rifle away from him. He could of killed us all."

"That you did, and thank you," Beth said. "I guess that makes you and Jack about even."

"What do you mean?"

"Well, Jack saved your life, and now you saved his. So you're all evened up."

"Oh...but, Jeez...we're in this together...aren't we?"

"Nope," I said. "You brought Grunt down here. Now you're on your own." I tossed the end of the line onto the other boat's deck as the two boats floated apart.

"But, but...." Bully sputtered.

"Come on Billy," Christina said. "Get a grip. There is no treasure. They want to get on with their visit without us, and I don't blame them. This is an OK boat. We'll just have to clean it up some."

"But, what if Grunt shows up?" Bully protested.

"We'll just have to get ready for him." She ducked down below. "First let's get rid of these damned ears." She handed out the jar of pickled ears.

Bully took the jar gingerly. "What am I supposed to do with this?"

"Over the side." Christina ordered.

Bully hesitated. "Grunt wouldn't like that."

"Billy! Dump them!"

Bully tossed the jar over.

"And here, all these porno videos have to go." She handed out a stack of video cassettes.

"Hey," Beth hollered over. "Is there a video machine on that boat?"

Christina poked her head out of the hatch. "Yes, that was Grunts principle entertainment. Watching porno flicks and cleaning his guns."

By the time we got underway there was a trail of trash riding the tide out of the lagoon. Christina was still passing stuff out to Bully who looked like he was starting to enjoy throwing things overboard.

As we motored by I waved and said, "*Au revoir!* Don't forget to keep an eye out for Grunt."

Bully raised his hand half heartedly and Christina waved from the companionway. "Don't worry about us. *Bon voyage!*"

I flinched as she handed Bully a rifle. He took it by the barrel and held it up questioningly. She jerked her thumb towards

Pacific Gold

the water, "Chuck it!"

"Right." He chucked it over the side.

"It looks like Bully has found a new Captain," Beth commented as we went out the pass towing Uncle Carlyle's out-rigger canoe.

"He could do worse."

"Do you think that we've seen the last of them?"

"I wouldn't bet on it, but I don't think that they will bother us at *Hiti*. I don't think they'd be able to make into the lagoon without the help of someone who knows the way."

"Can we make it in?"

I looked to where Uncle Carlyle and my cousin, Nga, (second cousin?) were standing on the bow sprint. They seemed at home on the water. "Yeah, with Uncle C's help I don't think we'll have a problem. He's been here since the war; he knows his way in and out of the lagoon."

"He made it sound kind of tricky."

"Well, I didn't say it would be easy." I put my arm around her. "I'm sure it's do-able."

She smiled up at me. "I'll settle for do-able."

There was a light trade wind blowing outside when I put up the sails and killed the engine. There was no hurry, high tide wasn't until mid-night. With the wind vane set, we all sat around on the sunny side of the boat and chatted. Now that Uncle Carlyle was used to the idea that we were kin he was full of questions-- mostly about people I never knew--and stories of way back when.

Later, with the moon giving us plenty of light. Uncle Carlyle stood on the bowsprit giving hand signals as we motored carefully through a very tight break in the reef that surrounded *Hiti* atoll and into the coral studded lagoon. We didn't touch bottom and anchored in three fathoms of water with enough room to swing.

Carlyle and his Grand-daughter paddled ashore while Beth and I crawled into our bunk for some much needed sleep.

Over the next few days we got to know twenty, or so, people living on the atoll. We were all related through Uncle Carlyle. Here was a whole group of cousins, second cousins, cousins-in-law, and other shirt tail relations that I didn't even know existed. I soon gathered that *Hiti* was only one of their homes and that most of the people only lived there when the feeling struck them. They came over to visit, to fish, to dive for pearls in the lagoon, and to make copra. Some more, some less. Uncle Carlyle and his wife, Raua, seemed to be full time residents with only occasional forays into the outside world. It was easy to see how Uncle Carlyle came to settle in. Arriving in such peace and tranquility from a war zone must have been heavenly.

It felt that way to me too; a safe haven after knocking around the ocean dodging Bully and then, the grand finale with Grunt. It would have been nice to have found the treasure, but it was OK this way too--except that we were broke.

"So now what?" Beth asked. We were sitting on Uncle Carlyle's back porch gazing out over the lagoon where Hispaniola floated quietly at anchor.

"Good question. I guess we could stay here and eat fish and coconuts, but I don't think that I'm really cut out for that life style. And then I suppose the French immigration might have something to say about it too."

"I guess we could sail back home, or at least to the U.S. and get jobs."

"I didn't really plan on going back to the old working world, but there might not be a choice.

Pacific Gold

It's too bad that there isn't any treasure to dig up."

"No treasure?" Uncle Carlyle had come up behind us unnoticed. He wasn't eves-dropping, he just didn't make a lot of noise when he moved about. "Who said there isn't any treasure?"

Startled, Beth turned to him. "Why you did. You said that you dug it up and took it to Europe."

"Yes, but I left some buried."

"But where?" I asked. "I haven't seen any sign of any airstrip on any of these atolls. Is there another island?"

"No, actually it's on *Tuanake*. But the air strip is long gone. The big hurricane in 1955 erased it and then the brush has grown over what little evidence of it remains." He paused, gently smiling. "If you want to do some digging, I can show you a good place."

"But why haven't you gone back and dug it up for yourself?"

"I've never needed to. Living here is cheap, and I brought enough money back from Europe the first time. No, I left it there in case it was needed. So now it looks like you could use some. Maybe this would be good time to dig up some more."

"It *is* back on *Tuanake* then," I said feeling the old excitement coming back.

"Oh God, *Tuanake*," Beth said. "What about Bully and Grunt and all that?"

"I hope that situation has resolved itself," Uncle Carlyle said slowly.

"That would be good," I agreed. "But there probably isn't any reason to hurry over there either. Maybe we should give them a little more time--there isn't any danger of them finding the treasure is there?"

"None." Carlyle affirmed.

CHAPTER 16: UNCLE CARLYLE'S STORY

• *2400 February, 21   Pos: Tuanake Lagoon*
Crs: ? Spd: 0   Dpth: anchored in 4 fathoms
Helmsperson: Carlyle
Comments: Tomorrow the TREASURE!

Uncle Carlyle's disclosure that there was more treasure, *and* that we could go dig it up, calmed our restless fears of total financial insolvency. We waited, just in case the situation over on Tuanake hadn't resolved itself. We stayed another two months on Hiti Atoll. Probably the only reason we acted then was a fear of losing all desire to move on--and rapidly expiring visas.

Life was that good there. We easily got into the uncomplicated routine of life on a small island. There were always many things to be done. But there was little urgency beyond the hunger in our bellies, the hunger in our minds,

Pacific Gold

and in our souls.

The first was relatively easy to fill, if occasionally a bit boring. There were lots of fish in the sea. Uncle Carlyle and his in-laws (our new relatives) knew how and when to catch them. There were coconuts in the trees. Even I could procure them. Those were the main stays--fish and coconuts. In addition there was usually someone around who made French bread in a coconut husk fired bee-hive oven. And Uncle Carlyle had created a garden on that sandy isle.

That provided one of the jobs. In the evening (when the heat of the day was dissipating,) we worked in the garden. It was one of the few tasks that we felt equal to the Polynesians in doing. We could haul debris and turn compost with the best of them, perhaps better as they didn't show much interest.

The mental hunger was easy to take care of too. Freed of our financial worries, our minds could explore the nuances of Tuamotan lifestyle. We delved into the mysteries and intricacies that made life here possible. It was fascinating to find the same qualities displayed that we had known where we had lived before. There were different rules and tolerances, but a lot of the same values and personalities. Still, there were intriguing differences. There was very little violence, and what there was was public--and so, ritualized. Most of the people seemed habitually cheerful. The absence of TV may have been responsible for more traditional social behaviors. On the other hand in the relationship to other life forms there was a certain callousness which was hard to get used to. It disturbed me to see small children tormenting the hermit crabs on the beach--especially with their elders looking on.

Our souls were at peace. At first I was

concerned that I wasn't contributing enough. It seemed that these generous people were giving us everything and we had nothing to give in return. (Except entertainment as we clumsily attempted to learn their lifestyle.) Uncle Carlyle guessed my feeling. He brought it up in the context of his own experience and pointed out that our presence brought new stimulation to the island society, new leavening. It gave the indigenous people a chance to assess their own lives by teaching us. He also pointed out the pleasure it gave for them to be able to give to us. And finally that there were many levels of productivity among the people themselves. There were the ambitious and the slackards, and that it really didn't matter because we were living in a place of abundance.

As we became accustomed to island life and the actual digging up of the treasure became less important. It was like a bank account that we would draw on when we needed to. I understood how Uncle Carlyle might neglect to dig it up for forty or fifty years, it was there if he ever needed it.

Actually, it was this realization that spurred us back into action. I began to wonder if, after forty or fifty years, Carlyle would still be able to find the spot. After all the air strip had washed away, these atolls were really no more stable than the Oregon coast. The ocean and the weather continually made little changes, which slowly added up to big changes and one day your house falls into the ocean.

Beth and I talked it over and decided that if, Bully and Christina (and possibly Grunt) were still there, we'd just have to deal with them. So, Uncle Carlyle, Beth, and I set sail back to

Pacific Gold 181

Tuanake.

It was an easy inter-island day sail that felt especially good after not having left the lagoon for months. With a newly scrubbed bottom Hispaniola enjoyed it too. I think Uncle Carlyle enjoyed it the most. We chatted about our upcoming voyage to Tahiti and he thought he might like to join us. He said that our visit had stirred up his old wandering desires. That he might like a trip to the outside world before he got too old--maybe even to Oregon!

I said that we didn't really plan on returning to Oregon anytime soon. He said he wasn't afraid to fly in "them big aeroplanes." It wasn't the airplanes that I was thinking about, it was the changes in Oregon. Especially landing in Portland after fifty or so years in the Islands. But, *por que pa?* Why not?

We rode the incoming tide serenely into *Tuanake's* empty lagoon. The only sign of Marauder and crew was some shiny stuff on the bottom from Christina's house, or rather, boat cleaning.

We dropped anchor as the sun settled into the western sea. I mounted the bar-b-que grill on the stern pulpit and set the charcoal ablaze to cook the yellow fin tuna we had caught during the sail over from Hiti.

"So, Uncle Carlyle," Beth broke the comfortable silence as we sat around sipping wine after eating too much. "Tell us the story of the treasure."

He looked questioningly at her.

"We've heard bits and pieces, I'd love to hear the whole story."

Uncle Carlyle looked in my direction.

"Me too." I agreed, nodding.

"Wull...awright," (Undoubtably due to our influence, Uncle Carlyle was quickly reverting

Oregon English.) "But I'm gonna quit if you fall asleep."

"That's a possibility," Beth assented. "But if I do it'll be from too much fish and wine, not because I'm bored with your story."

Uncle Carlyle shifted around getting more comfortable on his boat cushion while I refilled his cup with French wine that we'd purchased from the Chinese store in Atu Ona. (They had filled our old empty bottles from a plastic five gallon jerry jug. It was very good.)

Uncle Carlyle's Story

I:

"First you have to unnerstand that war is a messy business. Beth that is; you already know that from Viet Nam, don't you John?"

I nodded. "Definitely messy."

"When you read about wars in books it seems like they're all planned out with definite goals and objectives, and things going according to some genius' master plans. But the truth of the matter is quite different. Anyway from my point of view there seemed to be a lot of going this way and that. And lots of people in charge acting on their own best ideas without a lot of regard for anybody else's best ideas."

"Which is a long way to get around to saying that someone decided that the U.S. forces needed a bunch of emergency landing strips scattered about the South Pacific. And me, being a SeeBee involved in the construction of anything anywhere, got a lot of free trips to some very out-of-the-way places. This here atoll being one of them. Now, the war never got here. And I doubt that this particular landing strip was ever graced by the touch of a set of aeroplane wheels; but it was here just in case. And, who knows, maybe some poor aviator

Pacific Gold

happened by here and had need of it." He shrugged. "I was just sent along to help build it."

"Naow," he turned to Beth again. "Another thing you must unnerstand is the way the military utilizes their people. Before I joined up with the Navy I was a logger, and a farmer, and a fisherman. So I knew something about operating machinery and boats and such--so the Navy made me shovel operator. Heh, heh.." He chuckled at his joke, I joined him out of principle but Beth looked puzzled. "A hand shovel, like a spade?" He explained and Beth smiled her appreciation.

"So, mostly I was a laborer on the pick and shovel gang. A lot of the guys resented that duty, but I liked it. I was young and strong and it was peaceful, honest, and for the biggest part, uncomplicated work. The officer would show me where and how much to dig and I would dig. It was surprising all the different kinds of holes they wanted dug or filled in."

"Well, *Tuanake* here was part of a grand tour of the Society Islands. I was digging as usual, working with the dozers. It was pretty easy leveling everything out, only problem was that this sand isn't nice and firm like Oregon sand, it's too soft for an aeroplane to land on so we had to beef it up with coral gravel. And on the ends where they would touch down we had to clear out the sand down the hard coral underneath. Then they would dump in loads of gravel to bring it back up to grade."

"The big equipment moved most of the sand, but there was always plenty for a guy with a shovel to do. Always is. Anyways, there I was at the south end of the runway straightening up the pit before they dumped the gravel in. (You might think that a few shovels full of sand in the bottom of the hole wouldn't matter, but if you do, you don't know the military.) I was squaring up the southeast corner when I uncovered what looked like a potato.

I says to myself, "Now that is odd." It was kind of a hobby with all the guys to be on the lookout for artyfacts from the old heathen days. So I bent down and picked it up. And was it ever heavy!" Uncle Carlyle waved his empty wine glass around. "And, and when I looked at it closely I could see that it was gold! And there was some markings on it. (I know now, that was the way them old Spanish guys in Mexico and South America marked their gold to show who owned it and what it was worth.) I quickly scratched around with my spade. I was right in the corner of the hole and had to be careful not to cause a cave-in. I uncovered three or four more potato looking pieces of gold."

"Just then a truck driver hollered down that it was good enough and to get out of the way so he could dump his load of coral gravel, shingle, (I think he called it,) in before anyone could say different."

"So, not having any choice, I kicked some sand over them golden spuds and climbed out. You can bet that I noted the position of things very carefully. The hole was filled in, the airstrip leveled off, and it was done; allemande left and on to the next."

II:

Uncle Carlyle stopped there. I refilled his cup as Beth urged, "What happened then? How did you get to be missing?"

"Well now, that's a whole 'nuther tale," Uncle Carlyle said and took a slow drink from his wine cup. "A whole 'nuther kind of a deal entirely." He paused and stared into his cup

Pacific Gold

before taking another sip.

"I guess it don't matter much now, but that's a deal I'm not terrible proud of. Guess it's all part of the story though, and, like I said, don't much matter any more anyway." He stopped again. We waited in silence while he collected up those long gone days in his thoughts. The water lapped quietly against the hull and the squawk of a disgruntled sea-bird came from the nearby motu. In these peaceful surroundings it was hard to picture a war.

"Well, about this time the war was heating up to the west. So they moved us that direction. Finally, we got to the Phillipines. Now there's a hell-hole if I ever saw one. Nasty hot, swampy, malarial infected kind of a place. That was where I came face to face with the actual war-- and I wasn't liking it's looks. It may be unpatriotic and all--I can unnerstand how maybe the Japanese had to be stopped, but wasn't there another way? Killing for peace just never made any sense to me. And then I really lost interest when I caught some kind of Gawd-awful jungle fever. I was digging as usual. No heavy equipment this time because we were working in a swamp. Trying to drain it we were. One of the Officers decided that it would improve things. What he couldn't be made to realize was that the swamp was at sea level and wasn't about to be drained unless we raised the whole damned island. But he couldn't be told nothin' by a lowly shovel operator so we was mucking about in this swamp.

It didn't matter too much to me because after a couple of days I got struck down with the meanest fever I've ever had. In fact I'd never really been sick before. I thought I'd die. (I guess that must have been when I wrote one of them letters home to Ma.)"

I and Beth nodded.

"Then too, things on the military front were going to hell in a hand basket. Them Japs was kicking our asses." He turned to Beth. "Pardon my French but that was the way it was. Oh it was a worry-some situation. Too sick to hold my head up--and hot. Mercy it were hot. I remember sitting on my bunk with my head hanging down, watching the drops of sweat fall from my nose and splash into a puddle on the floor." Uncle Carlyle shook his head slowly, as though it still hurt, and took a thoughtful drink.

"Then there was the constant artillery fire. Nerve wracking. If I survived the fever I thought the Japs would get me. That was the lowest point in my entire life."

"Then the order to evacuate came down. People were running around in circles saying this, saying that, doing nothing. So I decided that I'd evacuate myself. I guess I was just used to doing for myself. So I packed up my few belongings and hitched a ride over to the air field. I expected to find someone from the SeaBees there, but instead--as soon as I arrived--this Army Sergeant came a running up to me asking if I was going to Bora-Bora?"

"Now, I wasn't. But when he asked that question, images of paradise came back to me from when I was there before. It didn't take a second for me to decide that yes, that was indeed where I was going. "Yes, Bora Bora, that's me." He took me by the arm, drug me across the tarmac, and pushed me into that aeroplane. I guess he didn't notice, or care, that I was almost too sick to stand--I suppose that all he was interested in was getting people into aeroplanes and off his airfield. (And, I have to admit, he was damned efficient.)"

"I started feeling better as soon as we got up to an altitude where the air was a cooler--and not so damned humid. (The air in them jungles was so wet that there were plants that didn't even have to have their roots in the ground to grow. They could live off the air.)" he added with a look of disbelief.

"Well, I started to thrive soon as we got off the ground. I was still weak as a baby but my mind seemed to clear. It didn't hurt either that the pilot instructed all of us passengers to keep a sharp lookout for any Jap planes that might be around to shoot us down. If there was anything that I didn't want, it was to be shot down."

"So anyways it was a long, slow, uneventful flight. After the first half hour or so I dropped off to sleep and let the other fellers be on watch. I didn't wake up until the plane touched down on the runway that I had helped to build on Bora-Bora. The island had changed since I was there. It was crawling with G.I.'s, and Polynesian's from all the islands that were trying to pick up some of Uncle Sam's money or that were just curious. Anyway, no one was expecting me and I was left to my own devices which was just fine with me.

Before long I ran into a Polynesian that I had met when we were abuilding the airstrips. He saw right-away that I was sick and took me home to his hut on the other side of the island. We had to walk, and I don't know how I made it all the way there. But I have a suspicion that he may have carried me the last part of the way. A big strapping fellow with a heart to match, somehow, I think he knew what I hadn't acknowledged to myself yet--that I was through with war."

Uncle Carlyle took another slow, thoughtful, drink. "It's a funny thing about these people. You might think that they don't care about much, and they may not when it comes to material things like houses and property and such, but when it comes to friends it's a whole different story. They did whatever was needed to help me do, or in this case not do, what I thought was for the best. They helped me avoid the rest of the war. And in the process of that I met Raua, and later married her."

III.
Uncle Carlyle silently rolled a cigarette. Out of habit, he offered me the makin's and I declined. (Island etiquette, Beth called it. Everyone here seemed to smoke and sharing was a part of life.) Uncle Carlyle lit up and inhaled deeply, then slowly exhaled letting the smoke curl up into his watery old eyes. It was as though he was seeing those long gone days in the smoke.

"The world was a different place in those days. Very few engine powered boats. The islanders still used traditional craft with sail or paddle for power. With no compass or sextant they would set out for an island several days away; never a thought that they might not find it. Just throw a few drinking nuts on board, maybe some cooked pig or bread fruit or whatever was handy, and off they'd go. You know how these people are. They can eat more than three or four Caucasians can in one sitting, then they can go for a couple of days without eating at all and be none the worse for it."

"Anyway, as soon as I was able they loaded up a fair-sized outrigger canoe and we sailed off to more remote islands. The longer I stayed with the people the more I knew this was where I belonged. And I knew where there was enough gold for a stake."

"All I had to do was be patient and stay out of the way until the war was over. I thought I could figure out how to live happily ever after, after that. Especially if our side won. Either way I figured things would work out. So I lived out the war on the islands. It was a fantastic time. Uncertain and exciting." Uncle Carlyle paused and smiled, reflecting on the past. His smoke had burned down to a stub held between old brown nicotine stained thumb and fore-finger. He sucked out a last puff and tossed butt over the rail.

"I guess you managed it OK," Beth commented. "It looks like you've lived the life that you chose."

He nodded, "Yes, I guess so. Of course it hasn't all been roses--but there have been glimpses of heaven." He paused. "It has been a good life. I'm glad I chose it."

"To live the life you choose. That's a rare thing."

Uncle Carlyle studied her for a moment and then said, "Isn't that what you are doing? Didn't you choose to come here?"

"Hmmm...Yes, I suppose we did." Beth admitted with a smile.

Hispaniola rocked to a gentle whisper of breeze that came across the lagoon ruffling the water enough to distort the mirror image of the half moon reflected there. I poured more wine and Beth said, "So the war got over and you were free to come back and dig up the treasure?"

Uncle Carlyle nodded his head slowly. "When the war was over I was right here--or rather yonder there on the beach. I had told Raua about the golden spuds and we were happily living in sin, waiting for the war to end; so we could dig them up and not be worried about surprise visitors droppin' from the sky."

I sensed him smiling his sad slow smile in the dark cockpit. "I don't think the gold really mattered all that much by that time, but it gave us an excuse to do what we really wanted to do. There was no one else here, just her and I. As you know, her clan owns these three atolls, but even then they lived elsewhere most of the time. We lived like Adam and Eve if they could have stayed in Eden after they ate the apple. Life wasn't easy, but it was good and we had our little world to ourselves..."

He took a slow drink and then rolled a new smoke. He licked the seam carefully and placed it between his lips while fumbling in his shirt pocket for a wooden match. He ignited the match on a thick old thumb nail and gently held the flame up to the end of his cigarette. The unguarded flame was steady in the windless night. When he exhaled, the smoke drifted casually westward on the night air.

He chuckled at his memories. "Actually, the war was over for six months before we found out. How could we know? We didn't have any radio or telephone or anything like that. No one came by. We had been here about a year when a wondering Copra Schooner put in here. Of course we didn't have but a couple of bags of copra for him, but he had the news of the world for us. He told us all about the big bomb and the end of the war." He shook his old head. "It all sounded sad and tragic. We were glad it was over, but did it have to be in the first place? Then too, it signaled the end to our idyllic existence. Or so we thought. I was still young enough to need an excuse to do the things I really wanted to do. So, with the war over, it was time to get to work."

"I didn't know then that I could just live

Pacific Gold

here. I guess Ruau knew, but then her people had been doing it forever. I came from that different world. I still had a lot to learn. I had to have a *higher purpose.*" Shaking his head he tossed his cigarette butt over the rail--it hissed in the darkness when it hit the water.

"So as soon as the Schooner left, I started digging. It was a lot harder than I anticipated but I was young, able, and determined. Eventually we found sixteen ingots of Spanish gold. A fortune."

"Another Copra Schooner came by and we took passage back to Tahiti. I went on to Europe to sell some of the gold. While I was there I was determined to see the place. And I did, but the whole time I was thinking about these islands and Ruau."

"That's about my whole story. I came back to stay. Ruau consented to marry me and eventually we came back here. We found *Hiti* more to our liking as it was more isolated. I think I've always had a nagging worry about being a deserter." He paused and thought a while. "Or maybe that was just another excuse to do what I wanted to do. Possibly--very possibly."

Chapter 17: The Treasure

1200, March 1   Pos: About 30 mi W of The Sea Gull Islands
Crs: 270°   Spd: 4 knts   Dpth: O.S.
Helmsperson: B.A & J.A.
Comments: It's very good to be back at Sea!

"Yo hay -- we're bound away..." Or something like that. It might be an old song or one I just made up. Anyhow, we're out of here. Not that the Tuamotus are a bad place to be. "But the wind blows free and so are we." We're Tahiti bound!

The morning after Uncle Carlyle told us his story, we marched ashore, shovel in (my) hand. It wasn't quite as easy as advertised. First: we slept in, (possibly due to too much wine and conversation the night before,) so the day was already hotter than planned. Second: things *had* changed a bit in the intervening forty odd

Pacific Gold

years since Uncle Carlyle had been doing any serious digging outside of his garden.

The airstrip was, as Uncle Carlyle had said earlier, long gone. The big typhoon of '52 (or thereabouts) had started the work; the sea, sun, other storms, and brush had finished the job.

So, we never would have found the treasure on our own. But, even if the airstrip was still around, we wouldn't have found the treasure.

Uncle Carlyle had moved it.

It had been such a struggle to dig it up the first time that he'd been very thorough. There was more than he wanted to pack around, so he reburied part of it for future use.

All he needed to do now was remember exactly where he had stashed it forty (or so) years ago. As I said, things had changed a bit-- perhaps in his memory as well as geologically.

After a good breakfast of Spam & Eggs with French bread (untoasted) and coffee; we set out. Uncle Carlyle led, I followed with the shovel, Beth brought up the rear with water bottle and back pack (for the gold). At first it looked like we were making a bee-line straight for the treasure. After a few hundred yards of slogging through soft sand the thick brush cut off the sea breeze and the perceived heat index went off the chart.

Uncle Carlyle hesitated.

Not a good sign--understandable--but not good. Sweating profusely, we tromped around slapping mosquitoes as the bushes ripped at our bare legs and arms.

Finally Uncle Carlyle slumped down on a fallen tree. "Whew." He wiped the sweat from his face with the front of his shirt. "We should have gotten an earlier start."

I nodded my throbbing head in agreement and Beth passed the water bottle. "You OK?"

He took a long drink. "Wine makes a body thirsty," he commented with a wry grin.

After we'd all had a drink Beth got to the point, "So, where do you think it is?"

"Well, I don't rightly know," Uncle Carlyle answered looking perplexed. "I have a clear picture in my mind, but now things don't look like that picture."

"Can you describe the picture to us?" Beth asked hopefully.

"That's a good idea," I chipped in. "Pretend that we're on Hiti and you can't come with us. See if you can give us directions to the spot."

Uncle Carlyle looked thoughtful. "Ok, I don't know if I can now, but maybe." He stopped and scratched among the grey bristly hair on his head.

"Ow!" Beth slapped a mosquito on her thigh leaving a big bloody splotch. "Maybe it would help if we went down to the beach."

I wondered if she was being helpful or just trying get away from the bugs (which sounded like a damn good idea to me.) "God yes," I said jumping up enthusiastically. "Let's go back down to the beach and start over."

I led the way back through the brush and bugs to the waters edge, actually into the water where we splashed water on our faces and etc... The salt water soothed the mosquito bites and scratches.

"You know, I think it's lunch time," Beth said.

"You know, I think you're right. What do you say Uncle, let's break for lunch."

"Alright," he said absentmindedly. "I can't understand how it could be so different. I was just back to the spot a few years ago. Well, maybe ten or fifteen--but still..."

We piled into the dinghy and headed for

Pacific Gold

lunch, no richer and maybe just a little poorer than when we set out in the morning.

"OK," Beth said, after we had eaten and were comfortably (drowsily) lounging on the boat cushions in the cockpit. "Close your eyes and let us have that picture."

Uncle Carlyle leaned back against the cabin bulkhead and closed his eyes. He remained that way for so long that I thought he'd gone to sleep. I was about to do the same when his mouth opened and it wasn't to snore.

"I'm standing on the beach," he began in a trance-like monotone with his eyes still closed. "Looking inland. It's morning, the sun is behind me warming my back and casting a long shadow towards the bush." He paused. "My shadow points towards a tall tree, maybe the biggest tree on the island--it's a little to my left."

(Beth was writing the directions in the back of the ship's log.)

"I walk to that tree...then turn south...and walk along the top of the ridge until...until I come to another big tree." He opened his eyes and leaned forward eagerly. "That's what I forgot! There was another big tree, two big old trees. I wanted to bury it there at the second tree, but I couldn't because of the roots. So I went on another twenty paces beyond that tree in line with the first tree and buried it there! Yes, that's it!"

He jumped up ready to go but Beth stopped him and read the instructions back.

"Yes, yes, that's it." He was heading for the dinghy and I quickly followed. Beth swam ashore.

On shore we quickly lined up on the beach (making sure that we were parallel to the water,) and looked inland.

There was a long pause, then Beth finally

said, "No tree."

"No tree," Carlyle agreed.

"Right," I acquiesced. "And no shadow." I gazed up and down the beach. "So do you think that this is about where you came ashore?"

Uncle Carlyle peered up and down the expanse of sand. "I don't think it mattered. It was the tallest tree on the island."

We turned back and studied the tree line.

"When was the last typhoon that came through here?"

Uncle Carlyle looked puzzled and then replied, "Well, there was a big blow about ten years back."

"Maybe it was big enough to topple the biggest tree on the island?"

"Could have been," he admitted. "We were on Tahiti at the time. When we came back Hiti was a mess. We had to clean up and rebuild. Took a couple of weeks, but we were still finding things in the sand long afterward."

"OK, so if it was ten years ago, it would have been after you were here checking on the treasure. But the tree should still be here--just knocked down."

"Right," Beth eagerly chimed in. "*And,* if we stood in the same spot on the beach at the same time of the day the shadow would still point to the spot where the tree was!"

"Hmmm, yes." I considered that. "But it would have to be on the same day of the year to get the angle right."

"Oh... I don't suppose you remember the date?"

Uncle Carlyle shook his head, "I don't even remember the year."

"So much for easy..."

We stood on the beach gazing inland, trying to will a tree to rise significantly above the rest.

"In the picture." I turned to Uncle Carlyle. "Are the big trees on the ridge top?"

He closed his eyes to summon up his mental picture again. After several minutes he said, "Yes, I think so."

"So maybe, if we find two big trees on the ridge line that have been knocked down...we'll be in the right place?"

"Like the one where we stopped just before lunch," Beth said.

"Right, possibly the very same."

"Right....so where was that?"

We gazed inland, obviously none of us was eager to plunge back into the mosquito infested jungle to look for a fallen tree that *might* be the right one.

"Ok," I said. "What would be your best guess as to where on the beach you would have been when you looked inland and saw the big tree?"

Uncle Carlyle looked irresolutely up and down the beach.

"Did you have a hut?" Beth asked hopefully.

Uncle Carlyle brightened. "Yes by gee, we sure did. Good Girl." He patted her shoulder. "It would have been over here," he said as he set off with big strides at an oblique angle towards the tree line.

And we came upon the remains of a small thatched hut, the fire ring and a few scattered empty beer bottles were the most prominent features. "We still cook here when come over from Hiti," he explained.

"Alright," I walked to the waters edge and turned around. "If you came ashore here, the tree would be...where?" I pointed inland swinging my arm back and forth.

Uncle Carlyle and Beth joined me at the waters edge. He gazed inland and pointed with new certainty. "There."

Of course there was no tree standing there, or any other distinguishing landmarks. I studied the spot and then set out in that direction.

"Wait," Beth interrupted my concentration.

Irritated, I swung around, "What?"

She was digging in the back pack. "This might help," she said with a smile, and produced the hand bearing compass from Hispaniola.

"Yes," I said, instantly regretting my irritability and trying to regain my good humor. "Good idea."

I walked back to the spot and had Uncle Carlyle aim my arm again (hand holding the compass.)

"OK, let's try that again." We set out resolutely, single file (me holding the compass, Uncle Carlyle carrying the shovel, and Beth with back-pack, water bottle, bug spray, and who knew what other good ideas..,) to find the treasure.

It occurred to me that it was no longer strictly Uncle Carlyle's treasure. Now, since it was lost again--it felt to me that, if we refound it, it really would belong to all of us.

We reentered jungle and fought our way up the soft sand slope through the creepers and bushes and down palm trees and standing trees to the top of the ridge that made up the back bone of the motu. No big tree, up, down, or sideways. But I was mentally prepared for that. I didn't really expect Uncle Carlyle's calculations to be spot on.

"Well, what do you think? Left or right?"

Uncle Carlyle looked both ways and pointed. "South."

Pacific Gold

We set off to the left. We stumbled and staggered along through the sand for what seemed a long time before we encountered a tree that had been blown down.

"Alright," I said. "What do you think?"

Uncle Carlyle studied it, kicked it, and said, "Could be. Seems kind of small though. Kind of hard to tell with it laying down like this." He seemed disappointed with the tree for laying down on the job.

I studied the tree for awhile and then said, "I guess we could stand it back up, but it would be quite a job."

Beth slapped a mosquito and said, "Well, let's go on and see if we come to the second tree." (Obviously she didn't see the humor in my little joke. I admit there wasn't much, but humor was in short supply.)

And sure enough, a ways further on we encountered another big old tree that had been blown down.

"Alright, now what was it? Twenty paces further?"

"Right."

"Since you know about how big the steps were, why don't you pace it off Uncle."

Uncle Carlyle confidently took the lead counting out loud every time his right foot struck the sand. "...eighteen--and--nineteen--and--twenty."

He handed me the shovel and I eagerly commenced digging. I was still digging when darkness began to creep in. Deep down in a four foot by four foot hole I was sweating like a pig (do pigs really sweat?) The mosquitoes seemed to prefer the lower altitudes--or maybe it was having their prey confined. I stopped and leaned on the shovel wiping my face with the back of my hand, it came away bloody. "Has malaria ever been a problem in the Tuamotus?"

"Not that I know of. Plenty of it in the Phillipines though," Uncle Carlyle answered.

"That's comforting. So, do you think this is deep enough?"

"Yes, I'd say I buried it about four feet down, you must be at least eight."

"Jacky, don't you think it's about supper time?" Beth asked sweetly.

I thought about it for thirty seconds for effect and said, "Yeah, we can always come back tomorrow." I tossed the shovel out and then looked at the hole that I was in. It was deep and in loose sand. Any attempted to scramble up the sides would just cause a cave in and I really didn't want to undo the work I'd just done. "Anybody bring a ladder?"

"Wait a minute," Beth said. "I've got a rope, maybe that will help." She dug around in the back pack and pulled out a short mooring line.

"Good idea," I muttered.

She tied one end around a nearby bush and threw the other end to me. I gave it a tentative tug. It seemed a little spongy but it held, so I started pulling myself out trying to walk up the side and do as little damage to the hole as possible. I was, maybe, three quarters of the way out when the bush pulled out.

"Eeeyahh!!" I scrambled trying to claw the rest of the way out of the hole--but slid back in and ended up partially buried on the bottom.

"That always was a problem with digging holes in this sand," Uncle Carlyle observed. "Getting out without caving it in. You got to be careful, we nearly lost a man that way. Ol' Harvey was buried for about ten minutes afore we got him dug out."

"Well thank you for that timely bit of information."

"Now Jacky," Beth intervened. "If you'll throw the rope back out, I'll find something more substantial to tie it to and we can go home and have supper."

"Right." I started to search around for the rope. It was rapidly getting dark. I had mosquito bites on mosquito bites. I was scuffed up with sand sticking to me everywhere like a sugar coated dough-nut. And I couldn't find the rope. Finally I found the bush that it was tied to, dug that up with my hands and got to the rope. I jerked it out of the sand and it swatted me in the ear. "Yeow, goddamn-goddamn-goddamn!" I yelled and felt better.

"Now Jacky, take it easy. Going berserk won't help."

"It might," I muttered and threw the coiled rope out of the hole with maybe just a little more force than was absolutely necessary.

"Oof," Beth emitted as she caught it in the dark. "Damn, I wish I would have brought a flash light."

"Here, this'll hold him," Uncle Carlyle said.

I heard some more shuffling around and then, "OK Jack, look out here comes the rope." And it flopped into the hole beside me.

It was totally dark now, but the sky was just a shade less dark that the dirt. I stood up and tested the rope. Actually it wasn't *that* far. I could almost jump out. Maybe that made it even more maddening.

I tugged tentatively on the rope causing a fresh avalanche of sand. My hands were sore and my arms tired from shoveling all the sand out of this hole. Now they weren't eager to take the strain to pull me out of it.

But there was nothing for it. I spit out some excess sand, leaned back with my feet against the wall and started pulling with my arms. The sand started caving in immediately but I kept going, churning with my legs and dragging myself up with the rope. Suddenly I felt my feet against something solid. "Rock?" I thought. I stopped. "Can't be a rock. There isn't anything here except sand and coral boulders and they aren't smooth like this." I was about halfway up the side of the hole. I felt with my right foot and found a top edge to the smooth surface. "Hey! Uncle Carlyle? Did you bury the gold in a box?"

"Yes. I nailed it into an old dynamite box."

"Why Jack? What are you doing?"

I could almost see their two black forms peering over the edge of the hole.

"My feet are against something that might be a crate, or a box."

"I can't see a thing. What are you doing?"

"Making a seat." Holding myself up with my right hand. I passed the free end of the rope under my butt with my left. Then I made a bight in the rope just under my right hand and tied a one handed bowline.

That done I slowly flexed my knees and got with in arms length of the box. I could feel the rotting wood, "Yes, it's definitely a crate. I think we may have found it." I felt jubilant but didn't have the energy to show it.

"Really? Is it really it Jack?"

I pushed sand off the top causing more small avalanches. "I think it might be. It's definitely a wooden box." By the time I succeeded in clearing the sand off the top of the box, the rope was severely punishing my backside and shutting off all blood flow to my legs. I hauled up on the rope and stood on the box. "Could you hand me the shovel?"

"I can if I can find it," Beth replied.

"Here it is," Uncle Carlyle said and handed it over to me.

Pacific Gold

I cleared the sand away from behind the box throwing it into the hole. When I had cleared a space to stand I stepped off the box, turned around and attempted to pick it up. It started to crumble in my hands. "How heavy do you think this is?"

"Oh, probably not more than fifty or sixty pounds."

"Hmmm." I tried to pick it up again. No go, the box was falling apart.

"What's wrong Jack?"

"Ah, it's too heavy for the box."

"Could you take some out and hand it up?"

"Good idea." I carefully crouched over the box again. Little landslides were happening all the time and I was feeling anything but secure. I slowly, gently, wrenched a board off the top of the box. I reached inside. "Arrgh."

"What now?"

"The box is full of sand." I started scooping it out.

"Anything else?"

"Hold on," I dug around in the sand until my hand closed on what felt like a potato. A very smooth, hard, heavy potato. "Eureka." I said quietly, "This is it."

I carefully handed out those golden spuds one at a time to Uncle Carlyle, who passed them on to Beth, who secured them in the pack sack.

That done I scrambled out of the hole (it didn't cave in behind me.)

Uncle Carlyle helped me struggle into the straps of the heavy pack and we stumbled through the dark jungle behind Beth. Back to the beach and the boat and bed.

It wasn't until morning that we unpacked the treasure and lined up those old Spanish ingots on the cockpit bench that it really sunk in--we had found the Treasure! We admired them, took their pictures, hefted them trying to estimate their weight. Uncle Carlyle explained that the Roman numerals stamped into them was their weight in Libras--or hundredth libras-- or something like that. But it didn't matter because we didn't have any idea what a libra was and he couldn't remember. Our final analysis was that they were heavy and we didn't need all of them right now. So, we returned to the hole and reburied half of the potatoes for future use. Beth took careful notes as to where the hole was.

The day after that we sailed back to Hiti. There were only a handful of people in residence for our farewell feast (but it was a good one.) Then, with the tide, we set sail as a rooster crowed in the early morning cool.

So now we're westbound, headed-- presumably--towards a buyer for the gold. Perhaps we'll find him (or her) in Tahiti (or Hong Kong.)

"I wonder how Bully and Christina are doing?" Beth mused as we watched Hispaniola sail us through the blue water.

"Maybe we'll find out in Tahiti (or Hong Kong.)"

"Oooo," Beth shivered, "I hope not, I've had enough of Bully for a lifetime--maybe two."

"There is always a Bully. And what about Grunt? I can't believe that he is really dead."

"I can't either, all the time we were on *Tuanake* I had the creepy feeling that he was watching us. Maybe it was his ghost."

"Aye; *Grunt,the ghost of the Spanish Treasure*. I can't believe that he'd be the first though--he'd probably have to stand in line."

"You think so?"

"Sure the Spanish stole it from the Aztecs or the Incas or somebody in South America.

Pacific Gold

There's old blood on it for sure."

"Gee, I never thought of that. You're giving me the creeps. What if there's a curse on it? If it's stolen, maybe it *is* cursed. Maybe we have to have it Blessed or something? Maybe we have to give it back to its rightful owner?"

Another person might say something like that as a joke, (me for instance,) not Beth. She was serious. So I seriously considered it. "Well, aside from the fact that all those individuals are dead and gone by a few hundred years, and given that it was probably mined with slave labor, it would be pretty difficult to find a rightful owner. And Uncle Carlyle doesn't seem particularly cursed. Maybe the winds and rains of time have washed the blood off it." I wished I'd have kept my mouth shut about the treasure's possible history.

"Hmmm, I suppose so."

"I guess we could give it back to the Andes Mountains, they are the ones it was originally stolen from. Of course we'd have to go back to work ourselves if we did that."

"Yes, there's that. Maybe we could take a commission."

"What's that real estate term?"

"A Finders Fee!"

"Yes, that's it--a finders fee."

"I know who I'd like to give it to. The poor children who live in the Andes."

I thought about that for a minute. It sounded kind of sappy, but it sounded kind of right too. If anyone deserved a piece of the *Treasure* it was the descendants of the common people who dug it out of the mountains in the first place. Certainly not the priest-kings who profited from their labor, or the Spanish who stole it from them. "OK, I think we've got plenty, let's share it. We can stop in there on our way around the world."

"Good idea." Beth beamed at me.

"Yes, a very good idea." (Especially the part about sailing on *Around the World!)*

To Be Continued...

Pacific Gold

Made in the USA
Charleston, SC
06 May 2011